Praise for Cara Summers

"Cara Summers knows how to write fun yet passionate plots that readers will never forget."
—*romancejunkies.com*

"I can't wait to read more by Cara Summers."
—*The Best Reviews*

"Ms. Summers is a compelling storyteller with a gift for emotional and dramatic prose."
—*Rendezvous*

"With exquisite flair, Ms. Summers thrills us with her fresh, exciting voice as well as rich characterization and spicy adventure."
—*Romantic Times BOOKreviews*

"*Come Toy with Me* has a great plot, mysterious suspects, a wonderful romance, and lots of adventure."
—*Romantic Times BOOKreviews*

"Compelling plot, interesting characters, and plenty of heat make reading this book a delight."
—*aromancereview.com* on *Come Toy with Me*

"Mystery, adventure...a billionaire... what more could
—*Romantic Tim * de

"Ms Summers n
suspense and siz ss
that will have yo e
night...this is o need sunscreen for."
—*romancejunkies.com* on *Lie with Me*

Dear Reader,

I'm thrilled to introduce the second of my WRONG BED duets—*Twin Seduction*. Chronicling the misadventures of twin sisters Jordan Ware and Maddie Farrell has been a lot of fun...and a challenge of the best kind. Especially since both stories take place at the same time!

Maddie found her happily-ever-after with Jase Campbell in *Twin Temptation*. Now it's Jordan's turn....

Jordan's world has been shaken to its foundations. Not only has she lost her mother, but she's also discovered that she has an identical twin sister.

Then there's her mother's will. Eva Ware has left her design studio and business jointly to her two daughters— but only if they temporarily switch lives! Talk about a fish out of water. Jordan has to live on a working ranch for three weeks!

And the surprises just keep on coming. The biggest one happens when Jordan wakes up in bed with a sexy cowboy—Maddie's neighbor and would-be fiancé, Cash Landry—and realizes that she doesn't want to leave.

I hope you enjoy Jordan and Cash's story—and the sizzling attraction they can't seem to control. For news about upcoming releases, be sure to visit my Web site, www.carasummers.com.

Happy reading!

Cara Summers

Twin Seduction

CARA SUMMERS

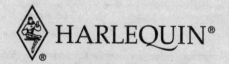

HARLEQUIN®

TORONTO • NEW YORK • LONDON
AMSTERDAM • PARIS • SYDNEY • HAMBURG
STOCKHOLM • ATHENS • TOKYO • MILAN • MADRID
PRAGUE • WARSAW • BUDAPEST • AUCKLAND

Recycling programs
for this product may
not exist in your area.

ISBN-13: 978-0-373-79484-3

TWIN SEDUCTION

www.eHarlequin.com

Printed in U.S.A.

ABOUT THE AUTHOR

Cara Summers has written more than thirty books for the Harlequin Temptation, Duets and Blaze lines. She has won several awards, including an Award of Excellence, two Golden Quills and two Golden Leaf Awards. This year she was also honored with a Lifetime Achievement Award for Series Storyteller of the Year from *Romantic Times BOOKreviews*. She loves writing for the Harlequin Blaze line because it allows her to write so many different kinds of stories—from Gothic romances and mystery adventures to romantic comedies. When Cara isn't creating new stories, she teaches in the writing program at Syracuse University.

Books by Cara Summers

To my lovely niece, Sarah Fulgenzi, a new June bride. Congratulations! I wish you a true "happy ever after," and I know you'll work hard to achieve it. I love you!

Prologue

WARE House.

Jordan gave the Long Island mansion a cursory inspection as she slammed the taxi door behind her. The overcast sky shrouded the place in even more gloom than usual. With its turrets and weathered gray stones, the three-story structure her great-great-grandfather had built looked as mysterious as ever. She'd always thought it could have served as the setting for the Gothic novels she'd enjoyed reading as a young girl. The kind of house that held lots of secrets.

At least that much hadn't changed. Because in the last week, everything else in her life had.

When pain squeezed her heart, Jordan rubbed her fist against her chest. *You've gotten this far. You can get through the rest.*

Seven days ago, two policemen had come to her apartment door with bad news. Her mother, renowned jewelry designer Eva Ware, had been killed by a hit-and-run driver as she'd crossed the street to her apartment building.

Her mother was dead.

A week had gone by and she was still struggling to accept that. Eva should be with her right now. They'd always come to Ware House together. But her mother wasn't here. She would never be here again.

Closing her eyes, Jordan ordered herself to take a deep

breath. She couldn't fall apart. She had too much to do. It would be her responsibility to make sure that her mother's legacy lived on.

A quick glance at her watch confirmed she was a good half hour early for the reading of her mother's will. She could take a moment to gather her thoughts, her strength. Turning, she began to pace on the flagstones in front of the huge entrance door.

You can get through this.

And she could. Hadn't she made it through identifying the body at the morgue and making arrangements for the funeral? Her Uncle Carleton and Aunt Dorothy had insisted on helping her with that.

Jordan had been both grateful and surprised when they'd contacted her because her mother and her uncle hadn't been on the best of terms for as long as Jordan could remember.

From what her mother had said, the little feud stemmed back to her grandfather's will. Carleton and Eva had each inherited half of Ware Bank, half of Ware House and half of his stocks, bonds and cash. Carleton had wanted his sister to invest her share in Ware Bank, the family business, but Eva had insisted on putting her cash into her fledgling jewelry design business.

To Jordan's way of thinking, it had turned out to be a wise decision since Eva Ware Designs was one of the most exclusive jewelry stores in New York City. Eva had tried to placate her brother's feelings by moving out of Ware House and letting him have the place to himself. Her Uncle Carleton, Aunt Dorothy and cousin Adam had lived there ever since, but the strain on family relations had never quite faded. Every time she and her mother visited, the chill in the air was so noticeable that her mother had rented a room at a small inn in nearby Linchworth when ever they intended to stay overnight.

In spite of all that, her aunt and uncle had been helpful in planning the funeral. Dorothy Ware had a great deal of expertise when it came to organizing social events, and Eva Ware's funeral had turned out to be just that. Thousands had come to pay their respects to the award-winning jewelry designer.

But the one person Jordan had wanted there hadn't been able to come—Jase Campbell, her apartment mate and closest friend.

She and Jase had first met during her freshman year at the Wharton School of the University of Pennsylvania. Jase had been a senior and they'd met by accident when they'd both shown up to rent an off-campus apartment. Instead of flipping a coin to see who'd get it, they'd moved in together and become fast friends. A year ago when Jase had left the navy to start up his own security business in Manhattan, they'd become apartment mates again. But for the last three and a half weeks, he'd been in some remote area of South America negotiating a hostage situation. She hadn't even been able to talk with him via cell phone.

He didn't even know that Eva was dead.

And he certainly didn't know about the other big change in her life. She'd acquired a sister.

Edward Fitzwalter III, her mother's longtime attorney, had called with *that* shocking news on the day after her mother's funeral. Even now, Jordan was tempted to pinch herself to see if the last week had been a nightmare that she could just wake up from.

She had a sister she'd never met. Madison Farrell. And she was coming here today for the reading of their mother's will.

Each time Jordan thought about it, her heart took a little leap and nerves knotted in her stomach. She'd only had two days to try to absorb it, and although she prided herself on her efficiency and adaptability, she wasn't sure she had.

How *did* one process the fact that one had a sister—an identical twin—who'd been raised all these years on a ranch in New Mexico by a father Jordan had never known? A father she would *never* know because he'd died a year ago.

The whole situation was straight out of a Disney movie. At first, she hadn't believed Fitzwalter. She'd nagged him until he'd shown her the birth certificates. She and Madison had been born in Santa Fe. She was older than her twin by almost four minutes.

Fitzwalter had also shown her a wedding license. Eva Ware had married Michael Farrell approximately eleven months before she and Madison had been born.

Immediately after seeing the paperwork, she'd looked Madison Farrell up on Google and begun a file on the sister she'd never met. Within an hour, she'd amassed quite a bit of information. Her sister went by the name of Maddie. In addition to being a rancher, her twin was an up-and-coming jewelry designer in Santa Fe. And except for a difference in hair styles, she and Maddie could have been mirror images of each other.

What would her sister be like? Would they have anything in common? From the looks of her Web site, Maddie had inherited their mother's genius for designing jewelry. Had Jordan inherited her father's talent for business?

Jordan sighed. Instead of answering her questions, her research had only brought more. Why had their parents separated them? Why had they been kept apart all these years? Why had her mother told her that her father died shortly after she was born? Would her sister have any answers?

Pushing back a fresh wave of frustration, Jordan whirled to glance back at the house. It still seemed impossible that her mother wasn't here right now. Today Jordan had faithfully followed their old routine, taking the train from Manhattan, then hailing a taxi. She'd even stopped in Linch-worth and checked in to the suite she and Eva always stayed in.

Why? Oh, she'd told herself it was so she had some-place to take Maddie after the reading of the will so that they could talk privately. In spite of her aunt and uncle's help with the funeral, she didn't think that the family dynamics had changed. But she wondered if she'd fol-lowed her mother's routine because she was having trouble letting go and accepting her death.

And what would Maddie Farrell make of the family dynamics? To say the Ware family wasn't close-knit was an understatement. Jordan rarely saw her uncle or aunt, and the only reason she saw her cousin Adam was because he worked as a designer at Eva Ware Designs.

The sound of a sports car roaring up the driveway drew her attention. Speak of the devil, she thought as her cousin Adam braked in front of the house.

Sending him a little wave, she marched up the steps. There was still time to get inside—depending on how quick Lane was to answer the door.

It had opened just a crack when a car door slammed behind her. "Jordan, wait up. I want a word with you."

Adam Ware sounded annoyed. Jordan couldn't remem-ber a time in the two years since she'd gone to work for Eva Ware Designs that he hadn't.

By the time Lane had fully opened the door, Adam was at her side. "What in the hell are you trying to pull?"

Jordan tamped down on her annoyance and sent her cousin another smile. "I'm here for the reading of my mother's will." Then she shifted her smile to the butler. "Good afternoon, Lane."

The butler, who'd always reminded Jordan a bit of Michael Caine, bowed slightly and stepped aside. "Ms.

Jordan, Mr. Adam, the family has gathered with Mr. Fitz-walter in the library."

"Has my sister arrived?" Jordan asked.

"Not yet."

"Your *sister,*" Adam snorted. "That's the very person I want to have a word with you about." He urged her through an open doorway to the left.

With an inward sigh, Jordan gathered what patience she could. Ever since she'd joined Eva Ware Designs, Adam had opposed every single marketing strategy she'd proposed. During the three years he'd worked alone with her mother while she'd pursued her graduate degree, her cousin had come to expect that he would one day take over and run Eva Ware Designs. And for some reason, her presence in the company had made him paranoid.

She'd tried to approach him on a rational level and pointed out that their talents lay in different areas—that while he brought his design expertise to the company, she brought a business background. But nothing she said or did seemed to assuage his fear.

Eva had mostly viewed the friction between them as a sort of sibling rivalry and gone back to work. But each time her mother had approved one of Jordan's marketing ideas, Adam had seemed to feel more and more threatened.

The spacious room Adam had ushered her into was furnished with antiques from the Victorian era. Velvet drapes in a rich shade of burgundy had been pulled back to allow in the dim light. When they'd reached the far end of the room, Adam turned to face her. Even in the dim light, he was incredibly handsome. He had his father's tall, athletic build, and his mother's rich chestnut-colored hair, worn long enough to push behind his ears.

"I want an explanation," Adam said in a tight voice.

"An explanation of what?"

"I want to know what you're up to with this sister you've manufactured. My father said that he'd received a call from Fitzwalter and that you're suddenly producing someone you claim is your long lost sister."

"I received the same call from Fitzwalter." Jordan worked to keep her voice calm. "I believe my parents are the ones who must be given the credit for producing her. Fitzwalter can show you the birth certificate. At my mother's specific request, he contacted Madison and arranged for her to travel here today because my mother wanted her here for the reading of the will."

"Why? Why reveal this second daughter now?"

Excellent questions, Jordan thought. "Your guess is as good as mine."

"I want to know what it means."

Jordan studied him for a moment. There was a hint of near panic in his eyes. "It means you have a cousin you never knew about."

He made a dismissive gesture with his hand. "That's not what I mean. I want to know how this person is going to affect my position at Eva Ware Designs."

"Very little, I would think." Adam wasn't the only one asking these questions, Jordan decided. He was probably only parroting his parents' concerns. She suspected there was a lot of parental pressure on Adam, particularly from his mother, to one day take over Eva Ware Designs.

"From what I've been able to gather, Maddie has her hands full running her ranch and her own jewelry-design business out in Santa Fe."

"She designs jewelry?" Adam's tone was incredulous.

"You can check out her Web site." She made a point of glancing at her watch, then turned to stride toward the door. "My sister is due to arrive any minute. So I think we ought to join the others in the library."

Before she could step into the hallway, Adam grabbed her hand and jerked her around. "You don't know any more than that?"

She met his eyes steadily. "No." Then she pulled herself free and led the way out of the room.

Lane was waiting down the hallway, and as they approached, he reached for the handles of the paneled double doors and pushed them open. As she entered the library with Adam a step behind her, the scents of lemon wax and lilies assaulted her senses.

Jordan paused for a second to let her gaze sweep the room. It was huge. Three walls were lined with bookshelves, and four stained-glass windows nearly filled the fourth. Fitzwalter sat behind a carved oak desk with his back to the windows. Red leather chairs had been arranged in two semicircles around the desk.

Cho Li, her mother's longtime assistant at Eva Ware Designs, had chosen a seat in the second row of chairs, and she returned the warm smile he sent her.

Uncle Carleton and Aunt Dorothy had already taken their seats to the attorney's right. Adam strode directly to them and said something to his mother. A report on their conversation, Jordan thought.

As always, she was struck by how handsome her uncle was. And how quiet. For as long as she'd known him, he'd been a man of few words. Her mother had always claimed that he was totally focused on Ware Bank, which had been established by his great-great-grandfather and whose branches were scattered all over Long Island. Considering her mother's focus on Eva Ware Designs, Jordan privately thought that brother and sister had a sort of tunnel vision in common. She wondered if Maddie would turn out to be the same way.

Carleton's hazel eyes were cool and shuttered as they

met hers. Jordan wondered what her uncle thought of the news of Madison Farrell's existence. Dorothy, too, for that matter. Her aunt was even harder to read than her uncle.

Jordan took her seat to Fitzwalter's left.

"It's two o'clock. Surely we can get started now." Dorothy Ware spoke in the same cool, unruffled tone she always used. As usual, her aunt looked as if she'd just walked away from a cover shoot for *Vogue,* but Jordan noted her hands were folded tightly on her designer bag.

Fitzwalter removed his glasses as his cell phone rang. Picking it up, he said, "Yes?"

After a moment, he disconnected the call, took his glasses off and said, "Ms. Madison Farrell will join us shortly. Her car has just pulled up."

A mix of nerves and anticipation jittered in Jordan's stomach. There was a part of her that wanted to dash out of the library and greet her sister at the front door. But there was another, more cautious part of her that was still struggling to accept what Fitzwalter had told her and what she'd seen when she'd examined the birth certificates.

Her sister. In a matter of seconds, she was going to meet her *sister.* How many times had she let herself imagine the moment? But this was real.

The grandfather clock ticked off the seconds. On the other side of Fitzwalter's desk, the Wares sat in silence, their eyes on the library door. Did they all suspect what Adam did—that she'd somehow conjured up a sister after all these years? Or knowingly kept her existence hidden?

A sudden spurt of anger had Jordan springing to her feet and turning to face the door. She'd had grown used to Adam's paranoia, but this was ridiculous. And her sister was about to walk into this frigid, hostile atmosphere. In her mind, she pictured Maddie entering the house, then following Lane down the long hallway to the library doors. Her own nerves paled in comparison with what she imagined her sister must be feeling. She started toward the doors.

When they opened, Jordan froze, and suddenly she and Maddie might have been alone in the room. As many times as she'd let herself imagine this moment, nothing had prepared her for the instant sense of connection and recognition that hit her like a punch in the gut. She felt winded—as if she'd just sprinted up a steep hill. It was one thing to see a photo on a Web site and quite another to come face-to-face with your mirror image.

Well, almost your mirror image.

Maddie Farrell had the same blue-violet eyes, the same facial features and hair color, but she wore a different hairstyle. Jordan kept hers cut just below chin length, while Maddie wore hers in a long braid just as Eva had done. How many times had she tried to convince her mother to switch to a more modern style?

Just as she had countless times in the past few days, Jordan pushed aside the little twinge of pain near her heart. She and Maddie had different taste in clothes, too. But Jordan liked the casual Southwestern style of Maddie's khaki slacks and embroidered denim jacket.

Jordan had no idea how long she and Maddie stood there taking each other in. Taking the reality in.

Everything that Fitzwalter had told her was true. She did indeed have an identical twin sister. And she was here.

And she was standing on the threshold like a deer caught in the headlights.

Jordan rushed forward and took her sister's hands. What she saw in Maddie's eyes—curiosity, excitement, anticipation—mirrored her own feelings so well. Once again, the sense of recognition struck her and some of her nerves settled. It was going to be all right. Whatever else happened, they were going to be all right.

Suddenly filled with joy, she whispered, "Welcome."

Then she turned to the others. "Uncle Carleton, Aunt Dorothy, Adam and Cho, this is my sister, Madison Farrell."

Cho rose and bowed. "It is my pleasure to meet Eva's other daughter."

There was one long beat of silence before Carleton Ware rose from his chair. "You'll have to forgive us, Madison. The shock of my sister's death coupled with the news that she had a second daughter tucked away all these years in Santa Fe…well, we're still trying to absorb everything. Until you walked in right now, I'm not sure that any of us really believed what Edward had told us. Dorothy, Adam and I want to welcome you to Ware House."

Jordan shot her uncle a grateful smile. For a man of few words, he could sometimes be counted on. Then she squeezed Maddie's hand and led her to a chair and whispered, "Once the will stuff is over, we'll talk."

1

THE SKY was still pitch-black when the limo pulled up to the JFK terminal at 6:00 a.m. When Jordan got out with Maddie, her sister turned to her in surprise. As she met her twin's eyes, she experienced that same odd sense of connection that she'd felt the moment she'd first seen her.

Maddie smiled. "Jordan, I can get onto the plane back to Santa Fe by myself."

"I know." Jordan led the way through the revolving doors of the terminal. "You must think that I'm some kind of control freak, not to mention a nonstop talker. But I still have some things to say. I'll walk you to the security check."

In the little inn in Linchworth where she had taken her sister after they'd left Ware House, they'd stayed up most of the night talking and talking and talking. But when Maddie had finally drifted off to sleep, Jordan's mind had replayed over and over the voice of Edward Fitzwalter III reading Eva Ware's extraordinary will.

Eva had left a sum of money to her longtime personal assistant, Cho Li. And to her brother Carleton, she'd left all of her shares in Ware Bank. Both of those bequests had seemed reasonable to Jordan.

Then Fitzwalter had gotten to the part that was going to turn her and Maddie's life upside down.

The rest of my estate, including stocks, bonds, cash, Eva Ware Designs, my fifty-percent share of Ware House on Long Island and my New York City apartment, I leave to my two daughters, Jordan and Madison, to be shared equally. It is my sincere hope that they will run Eva Ware Designs together. However, there is one requirement. They must change places and walk around in "each other's lives" for three consecutive weeks beginning within three days (seventy-two hours) from the time this will is read. If they refuse to fulfill the terms as I've set them out— or if they don't stay the course for three weeks—my fifty-percent share of Ware House will go to my brother, Carleton. Everything else, including the business and my apartment, will be sold and the profits divided equally among all my surviving relatives.

Her first reaction to the terms of her mother's will had been shock. Even her Uncle Carleton had been ruffled. Dorothy had said something to Adam in a low tone, after which he'd jumped from his chair and planted both his hands on Fitzwalter's desk. He'd insisted that there must be a mistake, that Eva had intended that he step into her shoes as head designer.

But there was no mistake. Her mother had wanted Maddie and her to switch places for three weeks, and she'd talked her sister into actually doing it. They were going to switch lives just as those girls had done in that Disney movie *The Parent Trap*.

Maddie had been reluctant at first, and Jordan couldn't fault her for that. Switching lives was going to be complicated, to say the least. But she'd explained that if they didn't fulfill the terms of the will, Eva Ware Designs, the company that her mother had devoted her entire life to building, would be sold. Jordan couldn't let that happen.

When they reached the escalator to the security check, Jordan drew Maddie aside. "I know I shoehorned you into this."

"You're not making me do anything I don't want to do. I've idolized Eva Ware ever since I was in junior high school." Maddie's brows knit together. "My father knew that and he never breathed a word."

"Mom never said a word, either. I've gone over and over it in my mind."

Maddie met her eyes steadily. "I know I was a little reluctant at first, but I understand that we can't let her business be sold. I feel the same way about the ranch."

Maddie had confided she was in a little trouble on that point. Ever since Mike Farrell's death a year ago, she'd been struggling to keep the ranch financially in the black. And lately there'd been some incidents of vandalism—cut fences, wandering cattle—and, more recently, an attempt to poison her horses' feed. A real estate agent, sniffing trouble, had been after her for the past six months to sell.

Maddie took her hands. "We only have to switch lives for three weeks."

To Jordan's way of thinking, that was the strangest part of Eva's stipulations. Why three weeks? She'd told Maddie it was something their mother had picked up from her personal trainer. Some behavior theorists believed that it took twenty-one consecutive days to build a habit.

Jordan squeezed her sister's hands. "You'll be careful and not stay late at work?"

"I'll be careful. I'll leave at closing time," Maddie promised.

There'd been a break-in and robbery at the Madison Avenue store about a month ago. The police were still looking into it. And Maddie wasn't used to the risks of living in Manhattan.

"I'll feel better when Jase gets back from South America," Jordan said.

"I'm more worried about you being alone on the ranch. I'll breathe easier when I know that my neighbor Cash Landry and my foreman are back from driving our combined herds to market."

One of the things they'd learned about each other during the brief time they'd spent together was that each had a guy pal as a best friend.

Cash Landry had been a part of Maddie's life ever since she could remember. He was like a brother to her—and a little overprotective at times. Jordan had described her relationship with Jase using nearly the same words.

"Cash may be back by the time you fly out the day after tomorrow," Maddie said.

"That reminds me. You've got your ticket for the return flight?"

Maddie smiled. "I do."

Jordan took a deep breath and let it out. "We can do this." And looking into her sister's eyes, she believed that they could.

"Don't worry," Maddie said. "I have the easiest part of this. All I have to do is live in your apartment and work in a jewelry-design studio. You have to survive three weeks on a ranch."

"I'll manage. I'm a quick learner."

"I have to go," Maddie said, releasing her hands.

For a second, Jordan felt the loss of contact. "You've got the notes I made."

"Right here." Maddie patted the duffel she was carrying over her shoulder.

"And I've got yours. And we'll talk," Jordan said. "Any questions, you just call."

"Right."

They moved toward each other at the same time, hugged, held on.

"Love you," Maddie said.

"Same goes." And Jordan realized that she meant it.

Then Maddie turned and stepped onto the escalator.

Jordan watched her sister until she was out of sight.

JORDAN TOOK one last look in her closet, then closed the door and checked her watch. 3:00 p.m. Glancing around her bedroom, she ticked things off her mental list. Her suitcase was packed. On the foot of her bed sat a stack of items still to be tucked into her open briefcase. And she had nearly an hour to wait before the limo service was due to take her to the airport.

Plenty of time for the nerves jittering in her stomach to have a field day. Jordan paced to the window and back. Had she been wrong to pressure her sister into agreeing to the switch? Frustrated, she strode to the window and stared down at the sluggishly moving traffic on the street below. She hated second-guessing herself. Usually, she never wavered once she'd made a decision.

But she and Maddie weren't the carefree preteens of *The Parent Trap*. They were adults with serious responsibilities. She really had no experience running a ranch, and Maddie had said that it was in a bit of financial trouble. But while she was there, Jordan intended to at least look into the business end of things and see if she could come up with a plan to help her sister out.

The easiest thing on her agenda would be to stand in for her sister at a big jewelry show where store owners would be placing orders for the next year. And she'd had an idea about that. She was going to impersonate Maddie at the show. She'd even purchased a hairpiece that she could fasten to the back of her head so it would look as if she'd tied her hair back into a bun. She was sure that potential buyers would be much more comfortable dealing with the designer, "Maddie Farrell," than they would be with Jordan Ware.

There wasn't a doubt in Jordan's mind that she could handle that side of the job. And Cho Li would be a great help to Maddie at Eva Ware Designs. But, well, her sister was going to be a fish out of water in New York City.

It wasn't that she was overly worried about Maddie's safety. Before they'd left Ware House, Adam had accosted them in the hall, and Maddie had actually shoved him into a wall. The shocked look on Adam's face was something Jordan would treasure for a long time. But living in New York City was a far cry from the life Maddie was used to.

If only their mother had given them more than three days before they had to make the switch. Then she could have eased her sister into the fast-paced life of the Big Apple. But thanks to their deadline, Maddie was going to have to face everything alone.

Jordan felt guilty about that. From the very first moment she'd seen Maddie framed in the doorway to the library, she'd felt this odd compulsion to protect her. Could it be simply because she was the older sister? For the life of her, she couldn't find a rational explanation for the instant sense of connection she'd felt with Maddie.

Jordan began to pace again. What choice had she had? If they didn't change places, Eva Ware Designs would be sold and the money divided among the other Wares, Maddie and her.

She simply couldn't allow that to happen. The business her mother had created and devoted her life to would have been destroyed. She and Maddie were doing the only thing they could do.

Moving to the bed, Jordan sat down again. She needed someone to talk to. And Jase wasn't here.

Jordan picked up a framed photo off the bed table. Jase had taken the picture at her college graduation. In it, she was fully decked out in her cap and gown and her mother was standing next to her.

"What were you thinking?"

It wasn't the first time she'd asked her mother that question in the past two days.

"And why in the world did you gamble the business you devoted your life to on an assumption that Maddie and I would go along with this ridiculous idea?"

At least Jordan had a theory about that. In addition to being a brilliant designer, her mother had been astute about people. And she would have known that Jordan would have been very tempted by the idea of living on a ranch for three weeks. Not to mention curious about the life her sister had been living all these years. And visiting the ranch would be the only way that she would get to know the father she'd been separated from.

But how could Eva Ware have been equally sure about Maddie, the daughter she'd cut herself off from all of these years? Had she kept track of the little girl she'd left in Santa Fe? Had her father kept track of her? Mixed in with the unending loop of questions was a keen sense of loss. In a way she'd lost two parents in the space of a week.

"Why did you and Mike Farrell get married and then break up? And why did you split Maddie and me up?"

Anger moved through her as she thought of the most important question—a question she wanted desperately to find the answer to.

"Why did you keep us apart all these years?"

It was unfathomable to her that her mother, a woman she'd thought the world of, could have kept her sister Maddie a secret all these years. And now there was no one to demand the answer from. Both Mike Farrell and her mother were gone.

Absently, Jordan rubbed at the little twinge of pain near her heart. Then rising, she moved to the foot of the bed and placed the items she'd previously stacked there into her briefcase: a guide to Santa Fe and the surrounding areas and a manila folder containing Maddie's notes on the people she might run into on the ranch and in Santa Fe.

Jordan had provided the same information to Maddie, but she'd organized it into separate files with photos. Her sister, like their mother, took notes on whatever came to hand—napkins, some pages from her sketchbook, the stationary from the bed-and-breakfast they'd stayed at after the reading of the will…

Last but not least, she bent down and grabbed a few well-worn paperbacks from her bookshelves. The books were all westerns by her favorite authors—Zane Grey, Louis L'Amour, Luke Short and Larry McMurtry. Guilt rippled through her. She was going to Santa Fe to make sure Eva Ware Designs went on to thrive. But she hadn't shared with her sister her lifelong obsession with ranches and cowboys.

She wasn't sure how it had begun, but there'd been a surprise Christmas gift from Santa when she'd been six. A miniature ranch, complete with buildings, fences, horses and, of course, cattle. She'd ignored the dollhouse her mother had given her and set up her ranch in a corner of her bedroom. How many hours had she spent reconfiguring those buildings and weaving stories in her mind about what life would be like on the range? And it wasn't long after that her mother had given into her pleas to take riding lessons.

Only Eva had known that she'd always fantasized about living on a ranch one day. It was a dream she'd never expected to come true.

But now it was.

When her cell rang, she reached for it and flipped it open. "Yes?"

"Hi. It's Maddie."

Panic bubbled up. Her sister should be en route to New York. "You've changed your mind? Look, I know I bullied you into this."

"You didn't bully me," Maddie said. "Maybe you plied me with some wine…"

At the humor in her sister's voice, some of Jordan's tension eased.

"I was late getting out of Santa Fe, and thanks to bad weather, my connecting flight to JFK is delayed here in Chicago."

"It's good to hear your voice." And it was, Jordan realized. Hadn't she wanted someone to talk to?

"Same goes. What about you? Having any second thoughts?"

"Not a chance. I'm packed and the limo is due in half an hour."

"We're really going through with this."

It wasn't a question. Jordan smiled and felt more of her worries and guilt fade. "Yes, we are."

"You remember where the key to the ranch house is?"

"Underneath the terra-cotta planter on the porch."

"And my latest designs for the jewelry show are—"

"In the safe."

"Sorry. Are you as nervous about me forgetting something?"

"No. All you have to do is consult the notes I gave you. And if you have questions, you can call me."

"Right. I've been thinking. Maybe Eva knew what she was doing. This is a good chance for me to get to know Eva and for you to get to know our father."

"It's our only chance." Something tightened around her heart. But Jordan knew that in business as in life, sometimes you had to play the cards you were dealt. And she was looking forward to learning what she could about her father.

"Would you believe it if I told you I'm looking forward to walking around in your shoes?" Maddie asked.

Jordan smiled. "Absolutely. Same goes for me."

It was the truth. And for the first time, Jordan believed that everything was going to work out.

2

EXCITEMENT WARRED with curiosity as Jordan drove the SUV into the small lean-to on the side of the ranch house. Thanks to the GPS system on her rented vehicle, she'd arrived safely at the Farrell Ranch in just under the hour predicted by the rental agent at the airport. So this was Maddie's home for the last twenty-six years.

It could have been her home.

The words had formed a chant in her mind ever since she'd stepped off the plane in Santa Fe. She could have been raised here instead of in Manhattan. Living in the wide-open spaces that she'd been driving through for the past hour wouldn't have been just a fantasy, it would have been her life. And she would have grown up knowing her father.

Although Eva had tolerated Jordan's love of horses, she'd never shared it. And now she'd lost out on knowing someone who would have. Why?

Jordan pushed down the surge of grief. This wasn't the time to indulge in it. While she was here, she would find answers.

So far, what she'd discovered was that everything—the landscape, the sky, even the air—was so different. On her drive from the airport, the rocks and sand had stretched away for miles on either side of the road. Unfiltered by even a trace of a cloud, the unrelenting light had bounced off her windshield and shimmered upward in a glimmering haze. Sunglasses had offered little protection against the blinding brilliance.

The hills in the distance had seemed so far away. But eventually, she'd reached them and begun the climb. The road had wound upward for several miles in a corkscrew. To her right had been the brownish rock of the hillside. To her left, the land fell away sharply at times into deep gulleys.

The vastness of the landscape awed her. She'd never seen anything like it except in her favorite movies.

Once past the hills, the road had flattened again, and as she drew closer, she caught glimpses of the ranch. The only building she'd been able to identify clearly was the house— a one-story sprawling expanse of stone, glass and wood. Now, thanks to the little bit of shade provided by the lean-to, she could finally get a closer look at the outbuildings.

To her far right was a long building, painted red with white trim. The stables, she guessed. Maddie must have a horse. It was one of many subjects that had never come up in the short time they'd spent together. She'd neglected to tell her sister that she kept a horse in a stable just north of the city. Jordan made a mental note to tell her the next time they talked. Julius Caesar would love it if Maddie paid him a visit.

Next to the stable sat a two-story structure that she supposed served as a bunkhouse. To her left and closer to the house was a smaller building—one story high and fashioned out of the same building materials as the main house. It had to be Maddie's design studio.

Then she let her gaze move to the land beyond the buildings. It stretched far into the distance, flat for a while, then gradually lifting into more hills. Something moved through her then. Was it envy that her sister could call this place home and she couldn't?

Ridiculous. She loved her life in New York. It had to be curiosity. And while she was here, she was going to satisfy it thoroughly by exploring every aspect of Maddie's life, starting tonight with the house.

A glance at her watch told her that she was right on time—8:00 p.m.

And she was stalling.

What in the world was she waiting for? Drawing in a deep breath, Jordan opened the door of the SUV and slid to the ground. The heat hit her like a punch, and she lost her balance as her heels sank into the sand. Slapping a hand on the side of the car, she steadied herself, slipped out of her shoes and tossed them into the car. Thank heavens she and Maddie had decided to share each other's wardrobes because her city clothes weren't going to serve her well in this new environment.

After grabbing her briefcase, she turned and stopped short. In the distance, the hills she'd just driven over were a stunning shade of orange as the sun dipped closer to their peaks.

She made her way, barefoot, to the trunk, muscled out her suitcase and circled to the front of the house. The ground felt hot and gritty beneath her feet, but at least she could walk. A wide porch with a railing stretched the length of the building. Before climbing the short flight of steps, she paused to study the house more closely. The intricately carved entrance door was framed by huge floor-to-ceiling windows that extended the length of the porch on either side. Whoever had designed the place had loved the land, Jordan decided.

And who wouldn't, she thought as she glanced over her shoulder to take another look at those brilliantly orange hills. There was a peacefulness here that appealed to her. Was it because she'd always had that secret fantasy about living on a ranch? But a fantasy was just that. She'd been born and bred in a city—with all its bustle and noise and constant excitement.

Still…there was definitely something about the place that was reaching out to her, tantalizing her.

Had her mother known that this would happen when she'd created that will?

Think about that later.

Knowing that she was stalling again, Jordan frowned and climbed the steps. It wasn't like her to be so hesitant. The key was just where Maddie had left it—under one of the terra-cotta planters. Jordan sighed and shook her head. No self-respecting Manhattanite would leave a key in such an obvious place. She'd had the foresight to give Maddie a whole ring of keys before her sister had flown back to Santa Fe the morning after the will had been read.

Very carefully, Jordan inserted the key into the lock and turned it. As she pushed the door open, she suddenly realized why an uncharacteristic caution had been dogging her ever since she'd convinced her sister to agree to the switch.

Whatever she was going to discover beyond this door, whatever happened to her on this ranch was going to change her life.

Drastically.

So be it, she thought as she strode into the room. But the feeling that moved through her was so surprising that she very nearly backed up onto the porch. The instant that she'd walked into the cavernous room with its steepled ceiling, she'd inexplicably felt at home.

TWO HOURS LATER, Jordan stood in front of one of the huge windows in the spacious living room of the ranch and watched lightning flash in the distance. The floor-to-ceiling windows offered a wide-screen perspective, and the display rivaled the Fourth of July fireworks in Manhattan's harbor.

It was nearly ten o'clock, and that meant it was 1:00 a.m. New York time. Still, she felt wired. After she'd finally gotten over her initial surprise, she'd been like a kid in a candy store, wandering from room to room, trying to take everything in. There were three bedrooms—a master suite she guessed had belonged to Mike Farrell, another one that probably served as a guest room and a third that definitely belonged to Maddie. The closet was full of her clothes.

Jordan had discarded her sweaty city clothes, taken a quick shower and then changed into a set of her own fresh underwear. Maddie's taste ran to plain white cotton. Hers never had. But she had borrowed her sister's robe. Then she'd spent the most time in a cozy room that served as a study or library. But everything she found raised new questions.

She glanced down at the photo of Mike Farrell she'd taken from a table next to his bed. In the picture, Maddie was on a horse. She looked to be about eleven or twelve. The horse was a beauty—black with white spots. Mike Farrell was standing next to her. Something tightened around Jordan's heart as she studied the images. Mike was handsome in a rugged, solid John Wayne kind of way, and he appeared to be a man who was comfortable in his own skin. His hand rested on top of Maddie's on the pommel of the saddle. There was something about the gesture that spoke of an easy camaraderie. And love. What had been the occasion for the photo?

Her mother had stood next to her in a similar fashion the first time that she'd shown her horse, Julius Caesar. They'd obviously loved their daughters. Or at least the one each had chosen.

Why had they separated Maddie and her? Why had Eva

and Mike split? The more the questions spun in her mind, the more determined Jordan became to find answers. Where had her parents met? Where had they lived when she and Maddie were born? Here on the ranch? If that was so, there might be someone in the area who remembered Eva Ware.

Frustrated and annoyed by the never-ending loop of questions, she strode into the kitchen. It was state-of-the-art, and the freezer and large pantry were well-stocked. Who was the cook, she wondered. Maddie? That was another question she'd have to ask.

But what she discovered when she opened the door to the refrigerator was that her twin was thoughtful. In spite of all the things that Maddie must have had to take care of to make the "switch," she'd taken the time to leave cheese, plump grapes and wine. A chardonnay from the same vineyard that they'd shared at the bed and breakfast in Linchworth.

Jordan tired to ignore the guilt she felt as she uncorked the bottle and poured herself a generous glass. Then she fixed a plate with brie and crackers.

She hadn't even thought about leaving food for her twin. Jase Campbell was the one who usually stocked the cupboard and refrigerator, and in the three and a half weeks he'd been in South America, she hadn't replenished anything. On her own, she either ate out or brought home take out.

That was probably not such a convenient option here on the ranch. After taking a sip of her wine, she picked up the bottle and the plate of food, then moved back to the window to watch the show. The lightning seemed to be closer now, and for the first time, she heard a faint rumble of thunder.

Good thing she wasn't afraid of storms.

But watching the show nature was providing wasn't going to relax her enough to sleep. Taking another sip of her wine, she moved to Plan B. A movie. She wasn't sure if it was Maddie or Mike, but she'd discovered earlier in her exploration of the library that someone shared her love of westerns. In spades. Not only was there an extensive collection of old paperback westerns, but she'd also unearthed a large cache of old cowboy movies. She'd run her fingers over the Clint Eastwood classics *Pale Rider* and *The Unforgiven,* before settling on one of her all-time favorites, *The Big Country,* with Gregory Peck. The movie centered on ranchers feuding over access to a river that meant the survival of their cattle, but there was also a strong love story.

A perfect way to end her day. Setting her food and wine on the big coffee table, Jordan lit a fat white candle and used the remote to turn on the big flat-panel TV. Finally, she settled herself comfortably on the leather couch and started the film. She couldn't prevent a smile as the movie's familiar theme music filled the room.

When the rumbling thunder drew closer, she merely upped the volume, took another sip of her wine and spread brie on a cracker. Within minutes, she was swept away to the ranch in the midst of the vast land that served as the setting for the movie.

THE STORM was finally tapering off when Cash Landry turned onto the highway. The sky was pitch-black, and the rain was still pouring down in sheets. Visibility was poor, but about an hour ago, the electrical fireworks had moved on to the east.

The problem was that parts of the road could be flooded, and there wasn't much chance of seeing that in advance. Bottom line, it was not the best time to be driving, but he had to check on Maddie. Mac McAuliffe, her foreman, lived several miles away with his family, so for the last year since Mike had died, Maddie had lived alone on the ranch.

Cash didn't like it. He liked it even less when he was out of touch with her as he'd been for the last ten days. His parents and then his father had been close friends with Mike Farrell, and he and Maddie had grown up together. Three years her senior, he'd early on taken on the role of looking after her. In his absence, he'd had his foreman, Sweeney, check on her daily when he came to feed the horses and check on the stock. When Sweeney had told him that he hadn't seen Maddie today, Cash had only delayed long enough to shower before climbing into his pickup and heading for the Farrell Ranch.

Truth be told, he was worried about her. Her ranch had been plagued by vandalism for the past few months, and the incidents had been increasing in frequency and severity. At first, he'd blamed the occasional cut fence on the Trainer twins. One of them—Joey—had an obvious crush on Maddie, and Cash figured he was making a bid for attention. He'd had a heart-to-heart with the boy. He'd explained that time was money on a ranch and that Maddie couldn't afford to lose manpower rounding up straying cattle and repairing fences.

But Joey Trainer had vehemently denied having anything to do with it. Cash had believed him. And there'd been other kinds of occurrences. Most recently, her horse, Brutus, had gotten ill. The vet had discovered that some of the hay had been poisoned. Since then, Cash had told Sweeney to bring over hay from the Landry ranch.

The most recent cut fence had allowed about a hundred head of her cattle to stray, and he hadn't had time to round them all up before he had to take their combined herds to market.

Pressing his foot on the brake, Cash turned onto the drive that led to the Farrell Ranch. When he hit the first rut and heard the water splash up into the undercarriage of his pickup, he slowed. The driving would be tricky from now on.

What had bothered Cash most was that whoever had poisoned the hay had come close to the house. Too close. So he'd taken to sleeping in the guest room a couple of times a week. It wasn't the perfect solution, but he was hoping that it would give whoever was behind the incidents pause.

Cash had his suspicions about who might be causing Maddie problems. Top of the list was Daniel Pearson, a real estate agent who'd been after her to let him put her ranch on the market for the past six months. Cash knew that Maddie didn't want to sell the ranch, but Pearson had been persistent, and he might believe that she would cave under pressure.

He'd checked and no other ranchers in the area were experiencing any problems. Only Maddie. Hitting another rut, Cash slowed his vehicle to a crawl. Ten days away had given him some time to think, and he'd come up with what might just be a solution to the problem, or at least a way to get Pearson to back off.

He and Maddie could get engaged.

He had to admit that when the idea had first come to him, it had given him pause. More than that, it had given him a good-sized jolt. An engagement hadn't been on his immediate agenda. It wasn't even in his five-year plan. He liked his life just the way it was. Being single suited him to a T. And he was pretty sure Maddie was happy with hers.

But it wouldn't be for real. Just a ruse so the incidents stopped until he could get some hard evidence about who was behind them.

Oh, his father and Maddie's had shared a lifelong dream of having the two of them marry and unite the two ranches. But it wasn't a plan that he and Maddie had bought into. Their relationship, even during their teens when his system had been hormone-driven, had never taken that turn into intimacy. Perhaps because he'd always thought of her as his kid sister and best friend.

But a fake engagement between the two of them wouldn't surprise their neighbors in the least. Most of them would think that Mike Farrell and Jesse Landry had been right after all. It shouldn't be hard to talk Maddie into it. He'd just lay out the logic of it and then give her a little push. Over the years, he'd learned that sometimes Maddie had to be pushed. Especially since she'd become so focused on her jewelry-design business.

Cash frowned as the dark outline of the ranch house came into view. The flood lights that normally lit up the stables and the house were off. And he couldn't see any other light coming from the house. The place must have lost power during the storm.

Chances were she was asleep. The last thing he wanted was to wake her up. But the more he thought about it, the more he wanted to talk to Maddie about the engagement thing tonight and get it settled.

Cash parked in front of the house. That was when he caught a glimmer of light. Some of his tension eased. She'd probably lit a candle. From the time she was a child, electrical storms had frightened her to death.

Not wanting to wake her if she was asleep, Cash didn't bother knocking. Instead, he looked for the key under the terra-cotta pot. When he didn't find it there, he frowned and some of his tension returned. He should have told her to find a better hiding place.

His frown deepened when he tried the door and found it unlocked. He'd have to have a word with Maddie about that, too. He saw her the moment he stepped into the living room and felt a surge of relief. She was stretched out on the sofa, one arm flung over her head. The fat white candle burning on the coffee table allowed him to see the half-empty plate of cheese and grapes and the opened bottle of wine.

His lips curved. She'd probably decided to weather the storm with a little help from a good chardonnay. It was only as he drew closer that he sensed there was something different about her. What was it?

Puzzled, he studied her more closely in the flickering candle light. Perhaps it was the clothes—or the lack of them. Her robe had fallen open. Beneath it, she wore a silk-and-lace tank top that skimmed the tops of her breasts. The matching panties left long, slender legs and narrow ankles bare. Then he saw it. Her toenails were painted a sexy shade of red.

Awareness and heat rippled through him. Cash frowned and glanced at the hand that she'd flung over her head. Her fingernails were painted, too—in the same sexy color. This time the heat was sharper, and an image planted itself in his mind of that hand moving over his bare skin.

He shook his head to clear it. This was Maddie. What was the matter with him? Narrowing his eyes, he let them drift over her again. This time he noted her hair. That was different, too. She'd cut it. The long braid she'd worn ever since he could remember was gone. Spread out as they were on the leather cushion, the honey-colored strands of her hair looked as if some man had just run his hand through them.

When he realized that he wanted to run *his* hands through them, he fisted them at his sides. What in the world had happened while he was away? Had she had some kind of a makeover? That was the only explanation that occurred to him.

Much harder to explain was the way his body was reacting to her. Why would painted nails and a change of hairdo affect him this way? When he finally dragged his gaze from her hair, it froze on her breasts. She wasn't wearing a bra, and so he could see the nipples beneath the thin swatch of silk that covered them.

Heat didn't ripple this time. It punched through him as if he'd stepped from an icily air-conditioned room into the blazing New Mexico sun. His knees nearly buckled.

What in hell had happened to him on that cattle drive? He was still the same man he'd been when he'd left. Wasn't he? But something had changed. What was it? He couldn't remember responding to any woman with this kind of intensity. And he hadn't even touched her.

He wasn't going to, either. He'd come over here to see that she was safe. And she was. So he was going to pick her up and carry her into her bed. Then he was going to bed down himself in the guest room.

Still, Cash hesitated for a moment, wishing he had more of a handle on what was going on. Finally he moved toward her and lifted her up off the couch.

JORDAN WILLED HERSELF to sink deeper into the dream. In it, she was with Gregory Peck, the tall, quiet tenderfoot who'd just fought a duel to save her life. They'd ridden back to her place, both knowing that all the obstacles between them had been removed. After they'd climbed the porch steps, he'd lifted her to carry her through the front door and across the room.

She heard the sound of his footsteps, felt the strength in his arms. It was the first time he'd touched her, and her head spun a bit as sensations arrowed through her with such clarity. She was intensely aware of the hardness of his chest and the heat from the press of his fingers on her stomach. Flames licked outward from that spot until her whole body burned.

Every detail was so real. The collar of his shirt was

rough beneath her palm, the skin on his neck damp. And he smelled simply wonderful—a mix of leather and horses and soap. She nuzzled closer. She had to get closer. When he stopped, she lifted a hand to his face, absorbed the sensation of that firm chin, the sharply angled cheekbone. Then unable to resist, she ran kisses along the line of his jaw. She wanted to taste him. She had to taste him.

As if he'd read her mind, he turned his head until his lips were just brushing hers. For a moment, she hesitated, and she sensed that he was hesitating, too. She was tempted to open her eyes, to try to see what he was thinking. But she knew, didn't she? And if she opened her eyes, he might disappear.

She couldn't let that happen. She had to keep him here. Tightening her fingers on his face, she drew him closer and whispered, "It's all right. I want you to kiss me."

When he did, she pushed everything else out of her mind and let herself plunge into the pleasure. His mouth was so soft. Different than she'd imagined. His flavors were different, too. Dark and hot and dangerous, they exploded on her tongue, shooting through her with such force that she was suddenly filled with him. Everything inside her sped up.

Never had a dream seemed so real. But reality had never brought this kind of pleasure before.

When he drew away, she knew a moment of pure panic. Of aching loss.

"Maddie, I—"

She felt the name whisper across her skin. It registered for a fleeting moment, but her desperation to taste him again shoved any thought ruthlessly aside. "I want more." She needed more. "Make love with me."

As he lowered her to the bed and joined her, he kissed her again. She nipped his bottom lip and threw herself fully into the dream. This time, beneath the flavors she'd sampled before, she tasted hunger. Was it his or hers?

They had to break off the kiss again and again as they rid themselves of clothes. Each time their lips rejoined, they demanded more. Received more. Their hands, desperate now, touched, tormented and took. Pleasure escalated, and the fire between them blazed more fiercely.

In some dim, recessed corner of his mind, Cash knew that he shouldn't be doing this. He shouldn't be in Maddie's bed making love to her. She'd had some wine. He'd seen the half-empty bottle. And she'd been frightened by a storm.

He'd never been an impulsive man. It wasn't in his nature to throw caution to the wind. But this was different. She was different. And his grip on anything rational had begun to slip the moment he'd stood at the foot of her couch and felt that first incredible punch of heat.

No woman had ever aroused him that quickly or that fully.

When he'd kissed her, his system had been totally shocked. Never in his life had he imagined that her flavor would be this exotic, this addictive. Each time he sampled, he seemed to find something new. And now he couldn't stop himself from wanting more. Or from taking more.

His hands had taken on a will of their own, racing over her, touching, tempting, claiming. Hers were no less busy, and each place her fingers pressed or her nails scraped, he felt twin ribbons of fire and ice race along his skin.

Speed seemed to be a necessity for both of them as if, like greedy children, they had to grab all the pleasure they could before someone snatched it away. Desire hammered at him with sharp, piercing blows until the pain of not having her became so intense that he rolled her beneath him and drove himself into her.

She wrapped herself around him, matching his rhythm

so perfectly that they moved as one, driving each other higher and higher. Even when they reached the peak, they paused as if to keep themselves there. As if they *had* to keep themselves there so that they wouldn't lose each other. Finally, sharp explosions of pleasure shot through them and pushed them over the edge.

3
_____

As CASH drifted up through layers of sleep, he was sure he heard a phone ringing. From far away. Gradually, bits and pieces of reality settled into his mind. But the biggest one was the fact that there was a woman in his bed. She was pressed against him like a spoon, her back to his front. Her hair tickled his chin, and each time he took a breath, he inhaled that wild exotic scent.

Maddie?

Everything that had happened the night before flooded his mind. This was not his bed. It was Maddie's, and he'd never expected to be in it.

Opening his eyes, Cash became aware of several things. He could tell by her even breathing that she was still asleep. He was used to rising at dawn, but the strength of the sun pouring through the window told him that the day had a couple of hours' head start on him.

Gradually, as his senses became more alert, he realized that his arm was still around Maddie, holding her close almost as if he'd been afraid that she'd leave at some point during the night.

Cash frowned. Could that have been the reason for the very odd dream he'd had? In it, he'd been standing at an altar watching Maddie as she walked toward him in a white dress.

No. The dream had to have been triggered by the fact

that he'd spent the last few days deciding that he and Maddie should announce their pretend engagement.

And now that they'd become lovers, well, the fake engagement plan held even more appeal. It had become more logical, he told himself. But there was a little voice in the back of his head that told him he wanted an engagement ring on Maddie's finger because he didn't want her to walk away. Ever.

Which was ridiculous. He and Maddie had been friends since childhood. Cash could hardly recall a time that she hadn't been a part of his life. She would always be there for him, just as he'd always be there for her. Not that he was going to delude himself into thinking that their relationship hadn't changed. Drastically.

She stirred.

Cash lay perfectly still as she sighed and snuggled even more closely to him. He caught her scent again—exotic, different. Odd that he couldn't remember Maddie ever smelling quite this way. One of his hands still covered her breast, and he became aware of her nipple pressing into his palm. His body hardened and he realized he wanted her again with the same sharp hunger that had consumed him last night.

What he'd experienced had been unprecedented, and it had been with *Maddie*. Shouldn't there have been some sign that their relationship was going to change this way? For the life of him, Cash hadn't seen one indication.

For a moment he was tempted to lift her hair and wake her by nibbling on her neck. But he knew that anything he started he would finish. He'd already experienced firsthand her ability to destroy his control. And before they made love again, they had to talk. He needed to know that she wanted that to happen as much as he did.

For now, he'd content himself with just holding her.

JORDAN ALWAYS woke quickly, as if someone had thrown a switch. So she was immediately aware that she was not alone in the bed.

Very much not alone. A man's hand covered her breast and his erection was pressed firmly against her backside. Her naked backside. Ignoring the panic that was bubbling in her stomach, she kicked her mind into overdrive. The last thing she remembered was lying on the couch and watching one of her all-time favorite movie couples—Gregory Peck and Jean Simmons and the wonderful romance that had blossomed between them in *The Big Country.*

But the hand on her breast was very real, and it was currently causing her whole system to go into a meltdown. She'd never experienced anything like what she'd felt during the night with another man. Was that why she'd let herself believe that it was a dream?

Jordan prided herself on not being prone to self-deception. And the hardening erection at her backside was knocking the dream theory out of the ballpark.

For a moment, she closed her eyes. Okay, somehow on her first night in Maddie's house, she'd slept with a stranger. Mentally, she ticked off the reasons why that might have happened—she was under stress, she'd always had secret fantasies about cowboys and ranches and she'd had some wine.

Maybe years from now when she was one hundred, she would be able to look back on this and laugh. Right now, she had to get through this the best way she could and that meant finding out just who the man behind her was.

Removing his hand from her breast, she wiggled forward enough to put some distance between them before she turned and found herself looking into a pair of gray eyes gazing at her intently. Panic bubbled up again. He definitely wasn't Gregory Peck. But he was dark-haired and not just a little handsome. His face was just the way her hands remembered—lean, with sharp cheekbones and a firm chin. And if the rest of what she'd touched ran true to memory, he was definitely a hunk.

And there was that scent—dark, irresistible, with just a hint of danger.

"Maddie, are you all right?"

Maddie? For a moment, Jordan was too shocked to think or speak. She had to jump-start her mind.

Maddie? Of course, he thought she was Maddie. She'd been on Maddie's couch, wearing Maddie's robe. Drinking perhaps a bit too much of Maddie's wine. But who—

"Do you want an apology?"

"No," she managed. Maybe Maddie would, she thought giddily.

"Are you protected? I didn't use any—"

"I'm on the pill." Thank heavens.

He narrowed his eyes. "And you're sure you're all right?"

All right? Oh, she was fine. She was lying in bed with a man she didn't know, a man she'd had hot, sweaty sex with, and she wanted to do it again in spite of the fact that he obviously thought he'd just made love to her sister. Jordan managed a nod.

"Good. Because I've got something to say."

"Wait." She pressed her fingers against his lips, intending to set him straight about who she was. The sharp heat that arrowed through her froze her.

He took her hand away from his mouth. "I've spent a lot of time since I last saw you thinking about this. And I believe that the best way to deal with the vandalism problem you're having is for the two of us to get engaged."

"No." Jordan snatched her hand away, scrambled out of

the bed and raced for the closet to grab a pair of jeans. "We can't get engaged."

"Why not?"

"Because I'm not Maddie." Hopping on one foot and then the other, she struggled into the denim.

Seconds ticked by, and Jordan felt his eyes searing into her skin for every single one of them. She'd never been this intensely aware of a man before. Why did it have to be this man? She snatched a T-shirt out of a drawer and pulled it on. If he was waiting for more info, so be it. This was not a conversation she wanted to have while she was stark naked.

"Then who are you?" His tone was patient, even.

Turning from the dresser, she met his eyes and said, "I'm Jordan Ware, Maddie's identical twin."

He was looking at her in an intent way that made her think he could see right through her. Nerves jittered in her stomach.

"Maddie's twin."

"That's right."

His eyes narrowed. "Maddie doesn't have an identical twin."

Jordan planted her hands on her hips. "Yes, she does. We just found out about each other a few days ago. And as far as being *identical* goes, I certainly fooled you."

There was another stretch of silence, and Jordan could have sworn she saw something flash in his eyes. Acceptance? Amusement? Both? Whatever it was, he was taking this a lot more calmly than she was.

"I knew there was something different about you." Narrowing her eyes, she watched him adjust a pillow against the headboard and settle himself against it.

"Turnabout's fair play. Who are you?" But even as she phrased the question, Jordan suddenly knew. He had to be—

"Cash Landry."

"The neighbor." Her heart plummeted. Her knees would have buckled if a sudden spurt of anger hadn't stiffened her spine. "Maddie told me you were just friends."

"We were. We are."

Jordan waved a hand at the bed. "What we did last night goes beyond the parameters of simple friendship."

"I agree."

Unable to contain herself, she began to pace between the bed and the dresser. "She said that she thinks of you as her big brother. I thought your relationship was just like the one I have with Jase."

"Who's Jase?"

Though he hadn't moved a muscle, Jordan sensed danger. "Jase Campbell is my apartment mate. We've been friends since we first shared an apartment in college. But there's nothing…" She waved a hand again at the bed. "We've never slept together."

"Neither have Maddie and I."

"Until last night," she shot at him.

"But it turns out that I wasn't making love to Maddie. I was making love to you. And I want to do it again."

There was a note of determination in his tone that had Jordan throwing her hands out in front of her. "No way." She might have been more successful in keeping the panic at bay if she wasn't right on the same page that he was. And the way he was looking at her, she bet he was reading her like a book.

"You thought you were making love to Maddie, and then you asked her to marry you.

"No, I asked her to get engaged to me."

"Whatever!" Jordan waved a hand. "The proposal makes this whole situation even worse. I just met my sister a few days ago and since then I've slept with the man who wants to get engaged to her. Way to go, Jordan."

"Where is Maddie?"

"She's in New York City. We've changed places. It's a long story."

"I've always liked stories."

When Cash moved as if to get out of bed, Jordan's panic grew, and she started toward the bedroom door. "You stay right there. I'm going into the kitchen and I'm going to make some coffee. Then you'll have your story."

Cash rose from the bed and reached down to scoop up his jeans. "Sounds good."

Keep your eyes straight ahead. But before she made it out of the room, Jordan caught a good glimpse of him out of the corner of her eye. It was enough to trigger a barrage of sensations. Heat. Lust. Longing.

She could feel him grinning at her as she hot-footed it through the door.

CASH TWISTED the faucets to the off position and reached for a towel. After a ten-minute cold shower, his mind had cleared a bit. While he'd been in the same room with her, fantasies had pushed and then lingered at the edge of his mind. More than once, he'd been sorely tempted to scoop her up and tumble her back into bed.

After hanging up the towel, he pulled on his clothes and shoved his feet into his boots. He'd used the bathroom off what had been Mike Farrell's room so that he wouldn't run into her. And so he could think.

He had a lot of questions about the things Jordan Ware hadn't yet told him. Like who exactly she was, why she and Maddie had changed places and why they hadn't known about each other for twenty-six years.

It surprised him a little that he was leaning toward accepting that she was indeed Maddie's identical twin. It would certainly explain his response to her, but not once in all the years he'd known Mike and Maddie Farrell had he heard a hint of a sister. The story he'd been told was that her mother had died when she was an infant.

He had to wonder if his parents had known about a twin. His mother had passed on when he was twelve, but he figured she must have been aware of the situation. So must his father. But there'd never been a word spoken.

If Jordan Ware was telling the truth, why all the secrecy? Who had finally revealed the secret and why?

Exiting the bathroom, he heard the faint sound of running water from the direction of Maddie's bathroom. So he had a short reprieve before he saw her again. Good.

Cash strolled into the large, open space that housed both the living room of the ranch and the kitchen and headed straight for the coffeemaker. The carafe was still half-full, and Jordan had been thoughtful enough to set out a mug for him. Grateful, he filled it to the brim and took a long swallow.

He should have known that she wasn't Maddie. Why hadn't the change in hairstyle tipped him off? As long as he'd known her, Maddie had worn her hair long and in a braid. Either that or she'd twist it up into some kind of knot at the back of her head. She didn't like to fuss much about her appearance, perhaps a result of being raised surrounded by males. No manicures and pedicures for her.

Jordan looked as if she took quite a bit of time with her appearance. Probably had regular appointments for those nails. Had he simply not questioned the differences because of the way that Jordan had blindsided his senses last night?

Maybe. It was hard to be sure because he'd never experienced anything like Jordan Ware before. Her effect on him was baffling. But he was going to figure it out.

At the sound of a door closing, he took another quick

swallow of coffee, then turned and leaned his hip against the counter. To brace himself? If he'd had any question about how she'd affect his senses this morning, it was more than answered when she stepped into view and strode toward him. He felt an immediate snap and sizzle in his blood, and a hard tug of desire. Basic. Elemental.

"I tried to phone Maddie, but the phone's dead."

For a moment, Cash didn't answer. He was too caught up in absorbing her. In the sunlight pouring through the windows, he could see more differences between the women. Maddie's presence was quiet, perhaps more controlled. Jordan radiated a certain energy. And she was wearing makeup. He'd never noticed any on Maddie. Jordan's was subtle, but she'd done something to make her eyes seem larger, and her mouth was painted a soft shade of rose. Hunger stirred sharply inside of him. When he found his gaze lingering on her lips just a bit too long, he took another swallow of coffee.

"Did you hear what I said?" she asked.

Cash dug for what she'd said. "The phone's dead. I thought I heard it ringing earlier. It's what woke me up, in fact." He shrugged. "Lots of time service is intermittent after a storm. It's not unusual for it to go on and off for up to twenty-four hours."

"My cell doesn't work, either." She moved to the coffeepot, and her arm nearly brushed against his as she refilled the mug she was carrying.

Her scent was just what he remembered—flowery, exotic—and it rekindled memories of the hot, sweaty sex they'd shared. He was surprised at how much he wanted to reach out and touch just a strand of her hair. He wasn't sure whether to be relieved or disappointed when she moved to the other side of the granite-topped island.

Cash drew in a deep breath. Growing up on a ranch,

he'd had to learn to adapt and go with the flow. The weather changed, the price of beef varied. So he was just going to have to learn to handle Jordan Ware's effect on him. Problem was, he just wanted to handle her, period.

JORDAN SIPPED COFFEE and made herself meet Cash Landry's eyes across the expanse of granite. It had been a mistake to get that close to him. Especially when he looked so good. With that long lean body, that ruggedly handsome face and those intent gray eyes, the man gave the words *boy toy* new meaning.

And the fact that she was even thinking of him that way shocked her. She'd never been a boy-toy kind of woman, but the idea was becoming very seductive. She thought that she'd pulled herself together while she was showering, but as she refilled her mug, she caught his scent again— pure cowboy, soap and leather and horses—and she'd wanted to jump him.

Wasn't that what had gotten her into this mess?

Very firmly, Jordan reminded herself of the conclusion she'd arrived at while she was showering. She was going to treat this as a business problem—solve it and put it behind her. Boy toys were off the agenda. She and Cash Landry were not going to repeat the little scenario they'd enacted during the night.

"Does your cell work? I need to talk to Maddie."

Cash regarded her steadily over the rim of his cup. "I've never been able to get a signal on the Farrell Ranch. It's in one of those blackout zones. Why do you need to talk to Maddie?"

"Why?" Setting her mug down, Jordan began to pace. "I need to talk to her about you and me." She waved a hand. "Us. And what we did last night."

"Why?"

Jordan paused to glare at him. "Because I just slept with a man who wants to get engaged to her."

"I can explain that."

She raised a hand, palm outward. "I don't want an explanation. I just want my sister to know that I didn't sleep with you on purpose. I thought you were a dream. I have a weakness for westerns, and I was watching *The Big Country*—"

"Gregory Peck, Jean Simmons and the feud over the Big Muddy."

She stared at him. "You know the movie?"

"It was one of Mike's—your father's—favorites. Maddie didn't like westerns, so he roped me into watching it with him a few times."

"So it was my father who read all those westerns in the library?"

"Whenever he could find the time."

Something inside of her warmed. Then she refocused. "I want to explain to Maddie that it was because I was watching that movie that I had this dream."

"About me making love to you."

She fisted her hands on her hips. "No. I wasn't dreaming of you. I was dreaming about making love to Gregory Peck."

"I wasn't dreaming, Jordan."

She pointed a finger at him. "No, you believed you were making love to Maddie. And then you proposed to her. I just have to figure out a way to explain it to her."

"It seems to me that we were both victims of circumstance."

Jordan's temper flared. "I don't know about you, pal, but I don't like to think of myself as a victim."

To her surprise, Cash Landry threw back his head and laughed. The bright, infectious sound of it filled the room and had her anger fading. In fact, she barely kept herself from smiling. "What's so funny?"

"Us. This situation. And the fact that you're absolutely right. It's hard to picture you as a victim of anything."

"I don't think Maddie will see the humor in this."

Cash's expression sobered. "I told you, there's nothing but friendship between Maddie and me. I've never touched her, never even thought about touching her the way I touched you last night."

The words and the way he looked at her when he said them had little thrills rippling over her skin. And her concentration was fading. No man had ever affected her this way. He only had to be in the same room with her to make her want.

"And I don't think you have to explain anything to your sister. What happened between us can remain just that— between us. No one has to know."

Jordan ruthlessly refocused. She couldn't deny that the idea of not having to confess to Maddie appealed to her. "But what about the fact that you want to get engaged to her?"

"I'll explain that. But first things first." His eyes never left hers as he set his cup down on the counter and straightened.

For a moment, Jordan was sure that he was going close the distance between them. If he did... Her hand trembled and coffee sloshed over the rim of her mug.

Then he asked, "Do you cook?"

"No."

He sent her a slow smile. "It's a good thing that I do. While I rustle us up some breakfast, you can tell me all about how you and Maddie discovered that you're twins and why you're here and Maddie's in New York City. Deal?"

Jordan let out a breath she hadn't been aware of holding as he moved to the refrigerator and began unloading bacon and eggs. "Deal."

CASH WATCHED HER scoop the last forkful of food into her mouth. She'd only wanted toast at first, but he'd ignored her request and filled a plate with bacon and eggs, as well. She'd made a second pot of coffee, poured orange juice and set places for them on the granite island.

The pull between them hadn't lessened as far as Cash could tell, but they'd been able to work in harmony as they'd prepared the meal.

Jordan had told the story of the last few weeks of her life in a straightforward manner with no trace of emotion in her voice. He'd promised himself that he wasn't going to touch her, but when she'd spoken about the visit she'd received from the two policemen telling her that her mother was dead, he'd reached over to cover her hand with his, and she'd immediately linked their fingers.

She still hadn't pulled her hand away. Cash glanced down at their joined hands. Hers was delicate-looking, her skin paler than his. Maddie had calluses on her fingers. Jordan didn't. Holding her hand felt…right.

Shifting his gaze to her face, he studied her as she took another sip of coffee.

From what he could gather, she'd been going nonstop ever since she'd received the news of the tragic hit-and-run. He knew something about the success of Eva Ware Designs because Maddie had talked about the famed Madison Avenue designer. So on top of absorbing the shock of losing her mother, she'd arranged a funeral for a celebrity, taken over the reins of a business and then had to make sure her newly discovered sister was prepared to step into her shoes.

His admiration for her had grown with each new detail that she added to the story. But Cash was also worried. To his mind, the terms of her mother's will and the decision she and Maddie had made to fulfill them could be a recipe for disaster. What had possessed their mother to put them in this position? If something happened to either of them— or if either of them backed out of the switch before the three weeks had elapsed—three of Jordan's relatives stood to profit. A lot.

He knew that Maddie wouldn't have thought of that. He wondered if the possible danger had occurred to Jordan.

"So Maddie is alone in your New York City apartment?"

"As far as I know. I haven't been able to reach my apartment mate, Jase, because of the hostage rescue job he's on in South America. He doesn't even know that my mother died, let alone the terms of her will. If he comes home, he's going to have a big surprise in store for him."

Cash could sympathize fully with that. Jordan had been quite a surprise for him. "What's this Jase like?"

Jordan smiled. "He's great. He's a good listener, and he lets me use him not only to vent, but as a sounding board for new ideas that I want to try out at Eva Ware Designs. I couldn't ask for a better roommate."

Hearing her sing the praises of Jase Campbell was leaving a bad taste in Cash's mouth. Was he jealous? That was ridiculous. In spite of that, he wished that the man was there in the apartment with Maddie.

"So Maddie's on her own?"

Jordan frowned. "She won't be once she gets to Eva Ware Designs. My mother's assistant, Cho Li, and Michelle Tan, our receptionist, will take good care of her. And I printed up all these files to fill her in. I even included photos."

"How about the rest of the family? How do they feel about Eva's other daughter suddenly showing up?"

A little frown appeared on Jordan's forehead. "Not so good, I suppose. Uncle Carleton was civil, as always. My cousin, Adam, may give Maddie some problems at work. He was obnoxious at the reading of the will. He's a brilliant jewelry designer, and my mother admired his work. I think that's why he always thought he had a clear shot at stepping into her shoes one day and running the business."

"And he's lost that because in her will, your mother suddenly produced a daughter who's also a brilliant jewelry designer and left her half of the business."

Jordan frowned. "Yes. If we both live up to the terms of the will."

"Depending on how ambitious he is, he could pose a real threat to Maddie."

Her frown deepened. "Adam? I don't think so. Basically, my cousin is a wimp. After the will was read, he followed Maddie and me to the door and grabbed my arm. Maddie unfastened his hand and gave him a shove that nearly had him bouncing off the wall. I have no doubt that she'll figure out a way to handle him."

She tilted her head to one side. "She's smart, and she's not the pushover she seems at first. I had to really do some fast talking to persuade her to switch places. She thinks I should have all the money and Eva's design business."

"You don't agree."

"No. We're sisters. The fact that Eva Ware and Mike Farrell split us up and kept us apart all these years doesn't change that."

If he hadn't already decided that he liked Jordan, her statement sealed the deal. "Maddie's lucky to have you for a sister."

"The luck is mutual." She set down her mug. Then, as if realizing for the first time that her other hand was still linked with his, she withdrew it and crossed her arms on the counter. "Now I think it's your turn to answer my question. Why did you propose to Maddie this morning?"

Cash ran a hand through his hair. "I knew we'd get

back to that. There've been some incidents of vandalism on the ranch lately."

"Maddie told me about them. Cut fences and someone doctored the feed in her stable."

"Maybe she didn't give you a clear enough picture. The poisoned feed in her stable nearly killed her horse, Brutus."

"Brutus? That's her horse's name?"

Cash nodded. "Your father gave him to her for her twelfth birthday."

When Jordan simply stared at him, Cash asked, "What is it?"

"I keep a horse just outside of the city. His name is Julius Caesar. What are the chances?"

"You're twins. You may have been separated since you were babies, but that doesn't mean you don't have a lot in common."

"I suppose." Then she frowned. "What else should I know about the vandalism?"

"The last cut fence was timed so a hundred head of her cattle strayed just before her foreman and I were going to drive them to market. We didn't have time to round them all up and that's going to cost her money. Money that she can't afford to lose."

She studied him for a moment. "You don't think the incidents are random, do you?"

"Maddie's problems have all occurred in the past six months, and during that time, there's a local real estate agent, Daniel Pearson, who's been urging her to sell the ranch. I don't like his timing."

Jordan wasn't sure that she did, either. "Maddie told me that she was having trouble filling her father's shoes. I can understand that. I can't step into my mother's, either. But she doesn't want to sell the ranch. I promised her I'd try to help with that."

Cash's eyes narrowed. "How?"

Jordan's smile was wry. "Good question. How does a Yankee tenderfoot think she can solve her sister's ranching problem? But I am a business major. And I want to help. I'll need to see the ranch first. Take a look at the books."

"I'll take you on a tour day after tomorrow. The best way to see it is on horseback. Think you can handle Brutus?"

"Yes." He was taking her seriously. Something inside of Jordan softened. "Why would you think that I might come up with something?"

He shrugged. "Gregory Peck was a tenderfoot in *The Big Country,* and he solved the feud over the Big Muddy."

"True." She grinned at him. "Now finish explaining why you proposed to my sister."

"It's pretty well-known around here that our fathers always had this dream that one day Maddie and I would marry and join the two ranches." He raised a hand. "Maddie and I agreed long ago that wasn't a possibility. Our relationship never took the turn that yours and mine has. But if we put it out there that we were engaged, I figured people would believe it and since Maddie would no longer have a need to sell, that might put an end to the incidents."

Jordan tilted her head to one side. "I've heard of a marriage of convenience. So this was sort of an engagement of convenience?"

"A fake engagement of convenience."

"Would Maddie have agreed?"

Cash sighed. "Maybe. After some serious and figurative arm-twisting on my part."

Jordan smiled at him. "That's how I got her to agree to switch places with me. You're a sweet man, Cash Landry."

Color rose in Cash's face, but before he could reply,

they were interrupted by a sharp knock on the door. Jordan moved quickly and opened it before Cash could.

Although he couldn't have explained it rationally, he was relieved to see it was his foreman Sweeney standing on the porch. But once Cash noticed the sober expression on Sweeney's usually jovial face, his tension returned.

The tall man took off his hat and nodded to Jordan. "Mornin', Ms. Maddie." Then he shifted his gaze to Cash. "Glad you're here, boss."

"Problem?" Cash asked.

Sweeney's eyes never left Cash's as he nodded. "I finished with the stock, and I was on my way over here to check on Ms. Maddie the way you asked me to. When I passed by her studio, I noticed that the door was ajar. So I went in."

"What is it?" Jordan asked.

"I'd better show you," Sweeney said.

4

JORDAN ALMOST had to run to keep up with the men's long-legged strides. The look in the older man's eyes had triggered a cold dread deep inside of her. The sun beating down from a clear, steel-blue sky wasn't enough to chase away the goose bumps that had broken out on her skin.

Maddie's studio had been broken into? Why? And by whom? Had something been stolen?

She thought she'd steeled herself. In the past few weeks, she'd developed a skill for doing that, but when Sweeney pushed the door open and she saw the devastation, her knees nearly buckled and she couldn't keep from crying out.

The open shelving that must have lined the walls had all been shoved over. Boxes had been overturned, their contents scattered. Gems and silver wires littered the floor. And scattered over everything like freshly fallen snow were shreds of paper. Maddie's design sketches? Something in Jordan's stomach twisted. Eva had always pasted her latest designs on the wall over her workspace. Would Maddie be able to replace them?

Leaning down, she picked up a chunk of turquoise the size of a baby's fist. A quick glance around confirmed that other stones—garnet, lapis, tiger's eye, some even larger than the turquoise—had been thrown helter-skelter throughout the debris. They had to be quite valuable.

"Why didn't they take the stones?" she asked.

"Good question."

She hadn't even been aware that Cash was touching her until he gave her shoulders a squeeze.

"Take a deep breath."

She did and felt her lungs burn. Control. She reached deep for it. When the backs of her eyes began to sting, she blinked rapidly and carefully picked her way further into the room. Cash moved with her.

Her heart thudded painfully in her chest as she thought of her mother's studio, pictured Eva's reaction if something like this had happened to her. A flame of anger began to burn inside of her. While thieves had broken into the main salon of the Madison Avenue store a few weeks back, they hadn't destroyed the place.

Taking another breath, she said in a low tone, "We can't let her see this."

"She won't have to," Cash said equally quietly. "I'll call my housekeeper. Mary's known Maddie since she was a child. She'll gather some friends and they'll put the place in order. Her husband will have the shelves back up in no time. This can all be fixed."

"Good. Okay. We won't have to tell her it happened."

"Yes, we will. She has a right to know about this, Jordan. And we need to know if anything like this is going on in New York."

A ripple of fear moved through her. "You think she's in danger, don't you?"

"I don't know what to think. But I don't like the terms of your mother's will."

She looked at him then. He had a take-charge attitude that she was grateful for. In most of her relationships, including the one she'd had with her mother and in her job, she'd been the person who usually called the shots. She was relieved in this case that she didn't have to figure out everything.

As she turned back to face the piles of debris, a thought suddenly occurred to her. "The jewelry show—the one that's coming up tomorrow in Santa Fe. Maybe those pieces were what they were after." Panic jolted her system. "I told her I'd substitute for her at that show. She said the new designs were in the safe, but—"

Cash ran his hands from her shoulders down her arms and back up again. "They are in the safe. She keeps all her finished work there."

The relief Jordan felt nearly had her knees buckling again. She knew that. Maddie had told her that. She wasn't going to fall apart. She couldn't. Very deliberately, she let her gaze sweep the room again. Someone had done this to scare her sister.

Behind her, Cash moved to speak to the older man who'd remained outside. "Go back to the ranch. Let Steven and Mary know. Tell them I'll call them as soon as the phones come back on line. If you could pack me some clothes and bring them, I'd be grateful. I'll be staying here until we figure out what's going on."

"Yes, boss."

Jordan heard the older man's footsteps fade, but she was still focused on the destruction. She pictured her sister sitting at the worktable. Then she scanned the studio again. The carelessness of the destruction, the meanness of it jump-started her anger.

When the first wave moved through her, Cash said, "C'mon. We're getting out of here."

She turned to face him, temper blazing in her eyes. "We're not just going to repair this place. We're going to find the bastard who did it and make him pay."

"Deal," Cash said.

As JORDAN PUSHED off the speakerphone button ending her call with Maddie, Cash slipped his arm around her and pulled her close. She looked shell-shocked. And no wonder. The news in Manhattan was even worse than it was in Santa Fe.

The message light on the phone had been blinking when they'd reentered the farm house, signaling that the phone was working—at least temporarily. The message had been from Maddie, and the machine must have picked it up when they were still in bed. That had been the phone call that had awakened him. According to Maddie, Jase Campbell had returned. When Jordan had reached Maddie at Eva Ware Designs, Cash was relieved to learn that Campbell had been with her.

He'd thought for a moment that Jordan was going to lose it when she'd told Maddie about the vandalism in her studio. But she'd rallied. She was an extraordinarily strong woman.

Then Jase Campbell delivered the bad news from their end. Eva Ware's death was being investigated as a homicide. A witness had seen a car parked across the street and claimed that when Eva Ware had crossed to her apartment building, the car had been aimed straight at her.

On top of that, Jase believed that Eva's death might be related to the robbery at Eva Ware designs. In Cash's opinion, that news, added to the terms of Eva Ware's will, put both Jordan and Maddie in grave jeopardy. It didn't comfort him that Jase Campbell was on the same page on that score.

"She was murdered," Jordan said as she turned into him and laid her head on his shoulder.

He wrapped his arms around her. When she tipped her head up to meet his gaze and he saw a tear roll quietly down her cheek, he had a moment of raw panic.

He had no experience handling a woman's tears. After

his mother's death, he'd been totally surrounded by men. But he had to do something. Jordan had just been dealt a bull's-eye blow. When Maddie and Jase had given her the news, her face had gone ghost-white. Even now, her breathing was shallow.

Was she going to faint on him? Panic nearly swamped him again.

Easing away, he kept an arm around her shoulder as he led her to the couch. Once he had her settled, he strode back into the kitchen and pulled a bottle of Mike Farrell's single-malt Scotch out of a cabinet. Carefully, he poured three fingers' worth into a glass and drank one of them himself.

He recalled that when his mother had died, Mike had brought a bottle to his father, and they'd shared a drink.

It wasn't the same. He didn't kid himself about that. His mother had died after a long illness. Even though her passing had been anticipated, the loss had nearly leveled him. Jordan hadn't had time to prepare herself—not for the hit-and-run and certainly not for the probability that her mother had been murdered. Glass in hand, he strode toward her and sat down on the coffee table facing her. She still hadn't moved. Praying it would help, he pressed the glass into her hands and said, "Drink it."

It didn't make him feel better when she followed his orders like a robot and shuddered.

"I'm going to be all right," she said. Reaching for his hand, she linked her fingers with his. Who was comforting whom, he wondered.

"I'll be fine. I just need a moment."

"I know."

A second tear rolled down her cheek.

"Take another sip."

She did. "I thought my mother's death was an accident.

Inexplicable. Tragic." Jordan sipped again. "Maddie's so strong. I almost caved. She didn't. For a moment after they told me, all I could think of was flying back to Manhattan to help them find whoever murdered my mother."

Poor kid. She had to feel like Chicken Little with huge chunks of the sky falling on her head. She'd lost her mother, then discovered she'd been kept from her father and had a sister she'd never met. And now this.

"Do you think they could be wrong?" Jordan asked.

"How smart is this Jase Campbell?"

"Smart as they come."

"Then I'm betting he's right. Can he take care of Maddie?"

"Nobody better," Jordan said. "I'm so glad that Maddie is with him. She can lean on him, and he'll make sure she's safe."

That had been his own take on the situation. But it occurred to him that during her long ordeal, Jordan hadn't had anyone to lean on. That much at least, he could change.

Another tear rolled down her cheek. This time she rubbed it away, then glanced down at her hand. "I never cry."

Good, Cash thought. If he could just keep her talking, perhaps she could ride out the storm that was swirling around inside of her.

"If we go with the theory that your mother was run down on purpose, do you have any idea of who?" His own mind was racing. Her mother had been murdered before the will had been read. What if someone had not benefited as much as they'd hoped or expected? "Who in your family might have wanted her dead?"

Jordan shook her head. "No one. I mean, I told you that my cousin, Adam, always wanted to step into her shoes one day. But I can't see him doing something like that. His own mother is always complaining that he lacks spine." She shook her head again. "I don't know. I just don't know."

Tears were rolling down her cheeks now. Cash doubted she was even aware of them. Taking the glass from her hand, he lifted her, then sat on the couch and settled her on his lap.

The floodgates opened. Not sure of what else to do, he kissed the top of her head and simply held her close. When he felt her relax against him and her tears began to soak his shirt, Cash realized that this was better for her than the Scotch.

JORDAN WASN'T SURE how long her little crying jag lasted. It was as if someone had turned on an inner faucet and then just as suddenly turned it off. When Cash pressed a clean hankie into her hand, she blew her nose, then settled back into the crook of his arm.

Letting a shaky sigh escape, she listened to Cash's heartbeat sure and steady beneath her ear. He didn't say anything, and she was grateful for that.

As the seconds ticked by in silence, she knew she should move. All her life she'd stood on her own two feet. Because her mother had always been so focused on her art and her design business, Jordan had had learned to take care of herself at an early age. Oftentimes, she'd watched out for her mother, too. During the last few years when she'd worked for Eva Ware Designs, she'd done more than improve the store's profits. She'd also insisted that she and Eva have a steady lunch date every Wednesday afternoon. After lunch, they would take in a matinee, visit a museum or simply shop. Artists needed breaks from their work to recharge and her mother seldom took one.

Toying with one of the buttons on Cash's shirt, she thought about her relationship with Jase. She didn't recall ever using him to lean on, either. Oh, when he'd been around, she'd used him as a sounding board, but she couldn't recall him ever holding her like this. In fact, she couldn't recall anyone holding her quite like this. Had she ever let her guard down quite this far? Had she ever felt quite this comforted? Or comfortable?

A trickle of unease moved through her. She had things to do. She'd made a promise to Maddie that she'd handle the jewelry show tomorrow. To do that, she needed to look at the pieces Maddie had stored in the safe, and then she wanted to go into Santa Fe and check out the venue of the jewelry show. She simply couldn't stay here any longer.

One more minute, she promised herself. His arms were so strong. From her present position, she could see the sharp line of his jaw and his chin. Stubborn, she thought. In that sense, he was like Jase. She'd never won an argument with her apartment mate. There'd been a few draws, she recalled. She had a hunch that if she crossed swords with Cash, he would prove to be just as much of a challenge. This time, it wasn't unease, but anticipation that moved through her.

Enough. She drew in a deep breath, intending to sit up, but his scent distracted her. Why was it that she couldn't seem to get enough of it?

Time to move, Jordan. But first…

"I'm sorry," she murmured.

"For what?"

"For falling apart on you. I never do that."

"No problem."

Beneath her ear, his voice was a comfortable rumble. It reminded her of her dream.

Which hadn't been a dream at all, she reminded herself. She really, really had to get back to reality and what she still had to do today.

"You're a kind man. I want to thank—" When she raised her head and her mouth accidentally brushed his jaw, her heart gave one good thump and then skipped a beat.

His eyes were so close she could see blue flecks in the gray, and they reminded her of a deep shade of lapis. It occurred to her for the first time how small the world became when you were looking into someone's eyes.

There was something very important she still had to say. And to do. But for the life of her she couldn't seem to get a handle on it. Not when his mouth was so close that she could feel his breath on her skin. Not when his earthy scent of leather and sun and soap surrounded her.

"Cash?"

His hand slipped under her chin, tipping her head up, and it seemed the most natural thing in the world when his mouth closed over hers. His lips were so soft. They didn't demand. They merely caressed. More than anything, she wanted to sink into the comfort they offered and into that odd feeling of coming home.

Then, he suddenly changed the angle of the kiss, and Jordan felt herself swept into that same uncharted territory Cash had taken her to during the night. For a moment, she was incredibly tempted to forget everything else and to lose herself in him and what they could do to each other.

But what had happened during the night had been a fantasy, she reminded herself. And she wasn't the woman she'd been in her dream.

She pulled back. "We can't."

"Why not?"

"Because." His mouth was barely an inch away, his hand still firm on the back of her neck. *Focus, Jordan. Treat this like a business decision.* "I don't have time. There are things I have to do today. Maddie's jewelry show is tomorrow, so I have to look at her designs and then I want to go into Santa Fe and check out the hotel where the show is being held."

"The day is still young."

He wasn't arguing, she noted, not in any vehement way.

He was merely studying her in that intent way he had. And she was outrageously tempted to just shut up. But she had to get a grip. "My life is complicated right now. I have to focus on walking around in my sister's life. I shouldn't be sitting here. I should be taking her designs out of the safe and making sure that they're ready for that show tomorrow."

She had to get up off his lap and move. She always thought more clearly when she was pacing. But she couldn't seem to push away. The man didn't have to do a thing. He just had to *be* to seduce her.

"Look, you need to know something. What happened last night, the way I was?"

"Yes?"

"That was because of the fantasy I was weaving. I don't leap into relationships, especially sexual ones. Normally, I'm very cautious. You assumed I was Maddie. I was imagining Gregory Peck. We should just chalk it up to some strange anomaly caused by the storm and forget it happened."

"Now, that's a problem." He leaned close enough to brush his lips over hers. "I can't seem to get what happened out of my mind. Speaking for myself, I want it to happen again."

Jordan desperately tried to gather her thoughts. But all she could think about was that she was poised on a cliff and the plunge had never seemed so tempting. Nor so dangerous. Finally, she just went with a lie. "That's just it. You're only speaking for yourself."

"If last night was a fantasy, aren't you the least bit curious to find out what the reality would be like?"

She'd been right about the challenge of arguing with him. The real problem was that she wasn't even sure she believed in her side of the argument. She *was* curious. And his mouth was so close. She was pretty sure she felt her brain cells shutting down. "I…can't think."

"Good. Maddie and Gregory aren't here. Let's not either of us think for a while."

This time when his mouth took hers, it wasn't a caress. It was a demand. Passion flared as immediate and urgent as it had been during the night. If she'd thought that she'd exaggerated the experience in her mind, she was wrong. If anything, what she was feeling now was sharper and much more intense. Her pulse had never hammered this hard. And her body had never ached this desperately. His flavors, rich and dark, exploded on her tongue, and she wrapped her arms around him, demanding more.

Knowing that the wide windows allowed them no privacy, Cash lifted Jordan in his arms and strode toward the nearest bedroom. Everything she'd said had made sense. The woman had a real way with words, and he was developing a keen admiration for the way her mind worked. Under ordinary circumstances, he was a cautious man himself. He didn't start up casual relationships. Perhaps last night they'd both been caught up in a fantasy of sorts.

And thanks to the damn will, things *were* complicated. But what he was feeling wasn't rational. He wasn't sure that it was even controllable.

He wanted her, and she wanted him. In fact, the urgency that he tasted as her mouth moved on his had him nearly stumbling as he stepped inside the bedroom. Kicking the door shut behind him, he turned and steadied them both against it.

He wasn't going to take her to the bed. Not yet. He didn't want any lingering memories of the night before clouding what they were going to do now. As he set her on her feet, their lips parted and she slid down his body. He hadn't thought he could get any harder. But he did.

Fingers fumbling, they worked together to get her out of T-shirt, bra, boots and jeans. The panties came last. He took one step back as she hooked her fingers into the lace waistband, pushed them down over her hips. The instant she kicked the panties away, he stepped forward, trapping her against the door. His eyes stayed on hers as he took his hands on a slow journey from her hips upward to the sides of her breasts, her throat. Finally, he framed her face with his hands. "Say my name."

"Cash. Say mine."

"Jordan."

5

As if their exchange of names were a signal, Cash closed his hands around her hips and lifted her. She felt the brand of each long finger burn her skin. She wrapped her legs around him, arching into his hard length.

Desperation had built so quickly on the short walk to the bedroom. Hadn't she just told him that she wasn't like this? She'd never before plunged into a risky sexual relationship with a man. But *no* wasn't a word she could seem to summon up—not when there was such raw heat in his lips and certainly not when there was such a wildfire of need in her own body.

She struggled to hold him close when he pressed her roughly back against the wall.

"Now." She arched against him again.

"In a…minute." Using his weight to keep her in position against the door, he gripped her thighs and eased her back a bit.

She heard the rasp of a zipper. Oh.

His knuckles brushed between her legs as he unfastened his jeans and let them drop. Her breath stopped when that last physical barrier between them had been removed. But it seemed to take him forever to toe off his boots and step out of his jeans. Finally, the head of his penis was pressing against her, so hard, so hot. So close.

The sensations careening through her intensified. No one had ever made her feel this way.

Now. Right now. She wasn't sure if she said the words or thought them.

He gripped her waist, adjusting his position. Then he eased his support and let her sink onto him. As she took him in, inch by searing inch, the enormous pressure sent whirls of pleasure arrowing through her. Desperate for even more of him, she arched. He shoved her back against the door and thrust into her fully.

He began to move then, his rhythm fast, right on the edge of violent. She welcomed the speed and met him thrust for thrust until the climax ripped through her. Once again, he let her body drop. She hadn't thought she could take any more of him, but incredibly she did as he pushed into her a final time and found his own release. A second orgasm, even stronger and longer than the first shot through her.

Afterward, she clung to him. The room was silent except for the sound of ragged breaths being dragged in and released. She couldn't distinguish which was his, which was hers. He kept her braced against the door, and as her head cleared, Jordan figured that it was as much for his own balance as hers. The darkness in the room was broken only by the thin shafts of sunlight slipping through the edges of the drapes. As the moments spun away, she decided that she could be content to stay this way for a very long time.

What was it about this man that he could make her feel wildly desperate one minute and sweetly comforted the next? She was going to have to figure it out.

It was Cash who moved first. He tightened his grip on her. Then with one arm around her back and the other under her bottom, he carried her to the bed. He was still inside of her when he lowered her and settled himself on top of her.

And he was still hard.

Using all the energy she had at her command, she opened her eyes, and what she saw in his had the fever building in her once more.

"Again," he murmured in her ear. "You'd think that would have done it, but I want you again."

She could feel the proof of that as he hardened inside of her. Heat built once again to wildfire proportions. "Me, too."

He began to move, pushing in and pulling out. His rhythm was slower this time, but no less compelling. As the need began to build between them, she wrapped her legs around his and dug her fingers into his butt to pull him closer, deeper. Gradually, the speed built as they rode each other, moving as one until they both shattered.

Afterward, he rolled off of her, then slid an arm beneath her to pull her close. For a while neither of them spoke. Her hand rested on his chest and she could feel the gradual slowing of his heartbeat. Cash Landry was a man who was comfortable with long silences. She never was.

"It seems I was wrong," she finally said.

"About what?"

"I thought that I wasn't the woman you were with last night. It seems I was. I am."

"I can't be anything but grateful for that."

"Me, either. I guess."

He tilted her chin up then so she had to meet his eyes. "You guess?"

She frowned a little. "Well, we're going to have to figure out what to do about this—about what's happened between us."

He tucked a strand of hair behind her ear. "I vote for just enjoying it."

"I suppose we could do that. For the three weeks I'm here. As long as the ground rules are clear."

"Ground rules?"

Something in his tone had a ripple of unease moving through her. But surely, he had to understand. "Cash, we come from different worlds. At the end of three weeks, I'm going back to New York and Maddie's coming here. Whatever it is that we have will end then."

His eyes had that intent look again. "Why talk about the end when whatever we have is just beginning?"

"Because I like to know where I'm going. I need to know. I'm where I am today because I developed a plan and followed through on it to the letter. Can you understand that?"

"Life isn't as predictable on a ranch. Things happen that you can't foresee. The price of cattle goes up and down. A hard winter can make it difficult for the herds to find enough to eat. A dry spring can cut back on the water supply. I'm used to rolling with the punches and coming up with solutions on the spur of the moment."

"Well, we could think of our…relationship…as rolling with the punches, I suppose. As long as we agree that at the end of three weeks, we can roll with ending things between us. That way, we don't have expectations that might hurt us."

"What if the punch rolls us in a different direction?"

"It won't. My mother's business is very important to me, and I'm needed in New York, especially now that she's…not there. I have to see that her legacy lives on."

When Cash said nothing, Jordan's frown deepened. "I'm not going to get you to agree to anything, am I?"

He lifted the hand that was pressed against his chest and brushed his mouth over it. "I certainly agree that we should enjoy each other as long as you're here."

"And the rest?"

"Why don't we agree to disagree on the ending part?"

She studied him for a moment. There was just a hint of recklessness in his eyes—something that she hadn't seen before. And damn it, she was attracted by it. She was suddenly struck by the realization that no matter what they agreed to, this man was trouble for her. Hadn't he already made her discover things about herself that she'd never known before? "I'm glad you're not a client of mine."

"I can agree with that." He shot her a smile that was so charming she forgot she was annoyed with him.

"C'mon." He took her hand and pulled her from the bed. "You need to see Maddie's designs, and then we should head into Santa Fe so you can check out the venue for the show."

Her brows shot up. "You're awfully agreeable all of a sudden."

He turned to her. "The day isn't getting any younger, and if I stay anywhere near the bed and you, we may not make it into Santa Fe."

She said nothing because her throat had suddenly gone dry as dust. She was very tempted to grab his hand and pull him back into the bed. Or onto the floor. Had the man turned her into some kind of sex maniac?

He shot her that bone melting smile again. "However, I'm flexible. If you want to change your plans…"

When he took a step closer to her, she threw up both hands palms outward. "No. I need to go into Santa Fe."

But she held her breath until Cash grabbed his jeans and boots off the floor and left the room.

Then she nearly ran toward Maddie's bathroom. A cold shower. It would help her think and get her back on track. Hopefully.

JORDAN WAS FAIRLY CERTAIN that she had herself back on track when she climbed into Cash's pickup truck. First of all, she'd taken the time to open the safe and examine the pieces that Maddie intended to showcase at the jewelry show. There had been a wide range—from intricately designed silver belt buckles to delicate necklaces and earrings featuring the turquoise that New Mexico was famous for.

Maddie had clearly inherited their mother's talent for design. But like Eva, she might need help in the marketing department. Jordan intended to give it to her. She was already thinking of the best ways to display the pieces at the show.

"Buckle up," Cash said.

"Sorry," she said. "I was miles away."

"You have been ever since you opened that safe."

"I didn't know until I did how much talent Maddie has."

The moment she fastened her seat belt, he started the motor and turned down the long lane that led to the highway. The searing noontime sun pounded down and the air conditioner blasted out more heat.

"You don't design?"

"No. My job at Eva Ware Designs is marketing. I've made a lot of changes since I joined the business. I intend to come up with some ideas for Maddie while I'm here. For starters, she needs a total makeover of her Web site."

Cash said nothing. One thing she was coming to know about him was that he only spoke when he had something to say. So he probably agreed with her on the Web site. If he'd ever taken a look at it.

The first thing she'd decided during her cold shower was that she wasn't going to argue with him over anything that was nonessential. He'd suggested they take his pickup. Since who drove whom in which car into Santa Fe was very low on her list of priorities, she'd agreed. In fact, taking Cash's truck would give her a chance to study her sister's notes again. In Santa Fe she was going to have to pretend to be Maddie full-time.

It wasn't until she'd gauged Cash's reaction that she'd thought she just might pull the masquerade off. The way he'd stared at her when she'd joined him in the living room of the ranch had finalized her decision.

"You look just like her," he'd said.

She should. She'd tried on three of Maddie's more formal outfits before she'd made her choice. Then she'd selected the newest and most feminine pair of boots. In her opinion, her sister needed a serious wardrobe makeover. She'd had to constantly coax her mother into keeping her clothes updated, and it seemed that Maddie favored Eva in that respect.

Still staring at her, Cash had moved closer. "What did you do to your hair?"

"Hair piece." She'd pulled her hair back from her face and concealed the short ends beneath a braid that was twisted in a circle. As Cash had circled her, she'd caught his scent, fresh from the shower, and firmly put it out of her mind. "Once I talked Maddie into switching places and going along with the will thing, I picked it up in a wig store and had my hairdresser dye it to match."

"I've seen her wear her hair exactly like that." When he'd completed his circle and stood in front of her again, he'd said, "You're going to pretend to be Maddie in Santa Fe, aren't you?"

She met his eyes directly. There was nothing slow about the way his mind worked. She hadn't wanted him to try to talk her out of it, so she'd gathered her thoughts and made her case. "It will be simpler. And better for Maddie. I know a lot about marketing jewelry, but buyers at the show will have more confidence if they believe they're talking to the designer. Maddie gave me some notes so I have names and backgrounds on buyers she's dealt with before. And even without the wig, I fooled the man who told us about Maddie's studio."

"Sweeney. I forgot to introduce you."

"I'd just as soon you didn't. I'm only going to be here for three weeks. I think it will be easier all around if everyone just assumes I'm Maddie. I think I can handle the boutique owners. Maddie gave me some notes on their names and their stores. I'm really interested in seeing what I can do to help my sister improve her marketing. And I'd rather not have to waste time explaining that I'm her twin and the terms of the will and so forth."

"That might make it easier."

"And if we run into that real estate agent, Daniel Pearson?"

Cash had frowned at her then. "That might be trickier. He's been out to the ranch, even took Maddie out to dinner a couple of times."

Jordan's brows had shot up. "He's putting that much pressure on her?"

"He is. In fact, if we run into him, he might be so focused on getting you to list with him that you might be able to fool him after all."

As Cash slowed at the highway, Jordan twisted in her seat to get a look at the ranch. Even through the spew of brown dust the pickup was leaving behind it, she saw that the neat cluster of buildings in the middle of a vast open space with a blue sky overhead made a perfect picture for a postcard. Something she couldn't quite put a finger on stirred at the edges of her mind. And she experienced the same feeling she'd had when she'd walked through the front door.

Home.

Why? She'd only been a baby when her mother had taken her away. Had some memory of the place lingered deep inside of her all this time?

She shifted her perspective to take in the blue-gray hills in the distance, the miles and miles of grazing land. It was so vast, so beautiful. Her throat tightened with an emotion she couldn't quite put her finger on. Longing? What she was certain of was that she had to figure out a way to make sure that Maddie didn't have to sell the place.

"Would my father have ever considered selling off part of his land?"

"Never."

"I don't suppose he would have considered leaving here."

"Ranching to Mike Farrell was like a religion. I think he thought of it as his calling. It's a perception that a lot of ranchers have, my father included."

And you have it too, Jordan thought. Something tightened around her heart. "So if my mother thought that she had to leave here and go back to New York, my father wouldn't have followed."

Cash glanced at her. "My best guess would be no."

Jordan sighed. "I can't blame him for that. In a way, my mother's jewelry design business was like a religion, too. She had such tunnel vision about it. They came from such different worlds, I can understand why they split but I don't understand why they separated Maddie and me—and why they kept it a secret."

Cash's only answer was to reach over and run a hand down her arm. They were beginning the climb into the hills and to distract herself, Jordan tried to concentrate on the view. But her rebellious mind kept returning to Cash.

She glanced sideways at him. Sweeney must have brought him the clothes he'd requested because he was wearing a white shirt and black jeans. The belt sported a silver buckle that she bet was one of Maddie's designs. He'd rolled his sleeves up in deference to the heat and the white cotton contrasted sharply with the sun-bronzed color of his skin. She had a sudden desire to reach over and run her hand down the length of that muscled forearm. God, she wanted to touch him. To get him out of that shirt and run her hands very slowly over every inch of him. They hadn't taken much time to explore each other during their frenzied lovemaking against the door or in the bed. Clearly, she hadn't had nearly enough of him yet.

And what exactly was wrong with that? Just as long as she kept their relationship in the proper perspective.

Bottom line—anything that developed between them had a three-week expiration date. But that wasn't all bad. She'd never taken the time to have a fling in her entire life. She'd been too busy going to school and then planning the changes she'd wanted to make at Eva Ware Designs. Those goals had been her focus. But there was absolutely no reason why she and Cash couldn't enjoy one another while she was in Santa Fe. As long as it didn't interfere with her other plans.

Cash glanced at her. "Is there anything else you want to ask me?"

Jordan felt her face heat. Could he have read her mind? *Get a grip.* Turning her attention to the road, she saw that they had started their descent down an incline. To the right, the land began to drop away.

"I'm assuming because of the dates on the marriage license and the birth certificates that my mother spent at least eleven months on my father's ranch starting around twenty-seven years ago."

She frowned. "Of course, I could be wrong about that. But they married a good eleven months before Maddie and I were born—so the marriage wasn't because she got pregnant. You said you didn't know anything about me. Do you think your father might have? Could he have known that there were two of us at one time?"

"He never said anything, but that doesn't mean he didn't know about you. My mother might have known, too. Your father could have sworn them both to secrecy. I've been giving it some thought. Ranch life is pretty isolated. It's hard work, too. There isn't a lot of time for socializing. So very few people might have known about you."

"Can you think of anyone I could talk to who might have known about my mother and about Maddie and me?"

Cash thought for a moment. "Maddie's foreman, Mac McAuliffe, has only been working here for ten years. Sweeney was around twenty-six years ago, but he never had any call to come over here. I was only three at the time and pretty much confined to the house. But there's old Pete Blackthorn."

Jordan dug her sister's notes out of her bag. "I don't think Maddie mentioned him."

"She probably figured you wouldn't run into him. He doesn't stop by the ranch as often since your father died. They used to play the occasional game of chess together. I think Pete misses him."

"Where does Pete live?"

"He keeps a trailer in a park south of Santa Fe. But he's rarely there. Pete's spent his whole life as a sort of free-lance prospector. His great-great-grandfather worked some of the Navaho turquoise mines in the area. A lot of people believe that he has some old maps that were passed down in his family that show the location of some of the old mines. He certainly seems to find more than his share of turquoise."

"Is he the source of those beautiful stones in Maddie's studio?"

"He's her only source." Cash grinned. "Even when she was a kid, he used to bring her stones to play with."

"I'd love to meet him. Not just to see if he knows anything about Maddie and me, but I'd like to buy some of that turquoise for Eva Ware Designs."

"When I take you on a tour of the ranch the day after tomorrow, we might run into Pete. I've seen him frequently in the hills to the southeast."

Jordan sent him a smile. "Thanks."

"Are you up to riding Brutus?"

"I'd love to ride him."

Cash glanced in the rearview mirror and frowned.

"What is it?"

"We've got company. There's a van behind us that's coming up fast."

Jordan twisted in her seat. In spite of the brown dust Cash's pickup was leaving in its wake, she could see the van clearly. It was black with dark windows. Sun glared off them as it closed the distance.

Cash eased his foot off the gas and pressed the brake. "There's a couple of curves coming up that are tricky. No one familiar with this road would be driving that fast." He pressed the brake again. "Maybe he'll take the warning and slow down."

The van closed the distance to ten yards, then five, then three. "He's not slowing. If he wants to pass—" But he wasn't trying to pass them, Jordan realized.

"Turn around and hang on."

Jordan didn't argue. She had a second to absorb the way the land fell away to their right. Then the van rammed into their rear bumper.

The impact slammed Jordan forward into the seat belt and had the rear wheels of the pickup fishtailing wildly. With her heart in her throat, she listened to them spin. She couldn't scream, couldn't think. All she could do was grip the seat with one hand, the armrest with the other and hold on for dear life.

6

TIRES SCREAMED and the truck then skidded onto the narrow shoulder. Dust and gravel erupted in a huge fan. Cash gripped the steering wheel hard as it threatened to rip out of his hands. Easy, he told himself. If he pulled too hard to the left, he'd send the car careening into the rock face.

"That wasn't an accident," Jordan exclaimed.

"No. He's trying to run us off the road." Cash didn't even consider lying. The problem was, the bastard behind them had a good chance of accomplishing his goal. At this point in their descent, the road was a narrow corkscrew, all sharp with angles and little or no shoulder. There was rock on one side and drop-offs to the right, some more sheer than others.

Once the truck was steady again, Cash risked a glance into his rearview mirror. The road had flattened a bit, and the van had backed away.

Jordan twisted in her seat. "He's not so close. What are we going to do?"

Cash shot her a quick glance. "Hopefully spoil his fun. Want to know the good news?"

"Bring it on."

She was frightened, but she was holding together. Another woman—perhaps even Maddie—would have panicked by now. "In my reckless youth, I did a little drag racing on this very hill." More than a little, truth be told.

"So you know the road."

"Like the back of my hand." Even as he spoke, Cash pictured a map in his mind, just as he had as a teenager.

"So what's the bad news?"

"I know the road."

Two beats of silence went by.

"You've got a plan?"

"You bet." It was a risky one. He hoped to hell it would work.

"What can I do?"

"Keep your eyes on the van. I need to keep mine on the road."

"Done." She twisted in her seat. "He's about fifteen yards behind us."

A sign flashed by with a warning of the upcoming double S curve. Cash was happy Jordan didn't see it.

"I want to know when he's out of sight." He eased his foot down on the gas pedal.

"You're going faster?"

"Yeah. He's going to hit us again, but he'll wait until we're farther down the incline where the drop-off is steeper."

"Good to know."

He couldn't prevent his lips from curving. She was a trouper. "There are two possibilities."

"So he has two chances?"

"Not if I can help it."

"He's speeding up, keeping pace."

"Good." On the map he had in his mind, Cash pictured the two places on the road where the land fell away sharply. In the first, the ground plunged into a series of gulleys, each one lower and deeper. There was a chance of surviving. The second option offered a sheer drop-off. Nothing but air for about one hundred feet. Barring a miracle, death would be certain.

If the guy in the van was a pro, and Cash was beginning to suspect he was, he'd have scoped the route out and chosen his spot. The second one. Cash would have put good money on it.

But if his plan worked, neither of them would get that far.

He let his gaze drop briefly to the speedometer and saw the needle inch past sixty. He reminded himself that the truck wouldn't corner as well as the car he'd driven in his teens. Swallowing fear, he took the first curve at close to sixty-five. His fingers dug into the steering wheel as he fought for control. The truck teetered briefly on two tires. After three heart-stopping beats, the other two slammed back onto the pavement. Heart pumping, Cash tightened his grip on the wheel and steered the pickup into the next curve. As his adrenaline spiked, his mind cleared, and he fine-tuned the image of the downward spiral of turns in his mind.

"Where's the van?" he asked.

"Still with us."

"Good." He wanted his pursuer to keep pace. For now. In the most acute angle of the spiral, the back tires skidded, screeching on the asphalt. They slid onto a narrow line of gravel edging the drop-off and spun for an endless moment before gripping the pavement again. Then the pickup shot forward.

"Can you still see it?" Cash asked.

"No. Too much dust."

Perfect. Cash was banking on the driver having to slow for a bit. But he didn't glance back himself. Nor did he look to the right. He knew there would be nothing to see but air.

Eyes narrowed, body tense, he focused all his attention on the winding road, matching it to the map in his head as he zigged and zagged into the next two turns. He'd done this before, he reminded himself.

"There's a bump ahead," he warned Jordan. When the pickup smacked into it and shot into the air for a few seconds, the bottom dropped out of his stomach—just as if he were on a roller coaster. He recalled the thrill it had given him when he was younger. This time, he swallowed fear again. The truck slammed back onto the pavement with a bone-jarring jolt.

In seconds, they'd reach the steepest part of the incline. This was it. Gritting his teeth, he anticipated the next stretch. *Hairpin* didn't even begin to describe the curves. "Hang on tight."

"I still can't see the van. Oh, there he is."

Cash pressed his foot harder on the gas pedal. A sign flashed by. He knew it cautioned a speed of thirty. With luck, he'd make it through the first turns. If he tried to take the last curve at this speed, they'd skid off the road.

But he didn't plan to take that last curve at all. Just ahead, right where he'd been picturing it, was a wide circular area of the shoulder that had been cut into the rock face. It was the only section of the road where a vehicle could pull off. Timing would be everything. Sweat beaded on his forehead and he prayed that his maneuver would work.

He began to tap the brake just before the wide arc of shoulder came into view. When they reached it, he eased the pickup closer to the opposite side of the road before whipping his vehicle to the left and into a spin. Tires spit gravel. Holding on to the steering wheel for dear life, Cash let the momentum take them.

JORDAN WOULD HAVE SCREAMED if her heart hadn't been trapped in her throat. They were going to die. Her mind was numbed by the thought. Her life didn't flash before her eyes. What did was a stream of scenes blurred by the dust the truck was spewing up, each one freeze-framed for an instant in the windshield of the truck. One second a solid wall of granite was dead ahead, the next a dizzying spin of road. Then nothing but air. Her stomach plummeted, and before the images could flash by again, she shut her eyes.

When metal screamed against rock, she knew the end was near. Now she'd never get to know Maddie or her father. Or Cash. She felt the sudden lurch of the truck, knew that he was doing his best to save them. He was the last thought in her mind before the truck suddenly shuddered to a stop.

Cash's hand gripped hers. "Are you all right?"

"Yes." And it was true. She opened her eyes. The scent of burning rubber filled her lungs. It was real. They weren't dead. As her vision cleared, she saw out of the corner of her eye that the rock face was to their right and they were facing up the hill.

Then through the haze of dust, she saw the van lurch around the curve ahead of them—the same one they'd just taken. The back end fishtailed, sending the vehicle into a fast skid. It was a little like watching a movie, Jordan realized. For an instant as the tires spun, the car careened down the road sideways—the front facing the rock face, the rear end spewing up gravel on the nearly nonexistent shoulder.

"He took the curve too fast," Cash said.

Jordan caught the grim satisfaction in his tone. She might have said something then, but she couldn't take her eyes off the van. It was still about fifteen yards away them when the tires found traction. For one horrifying moment, the vehicle shot forward, and she was sure it would crash into the granite wall. But at the last moment, the driver avoided the collision, by jerking the van back onto the road.

"He's overcompensating," Cash murmured.

As if to prove the point, the van tipped crazily to one side, the roof kissing the rock face and sending off sparks.

Then the vehicle careened forward, weaving drunkenly down the road.

"He's not going to make it," Cash predicted.

He was right. The driver had clearly lost control, and he was going way too fast. As the van whipped toward them, it shimmied and shuddered. When it tore past them, she and Cash both twisted in their seats. Together they watched it shoot sideways into the air at the side of the road. There was a sudden and complete silence, and for a moment, as it hovered in space, Jordan half expected the vehicle to fly.

Then, as if a magician had waved a wand, the front end pointed downward and it plummeted out of sight. The sound of the impact shattered the silence.

Releasing her hand, Cash unfastened his seat belt and opened the door. "Stay here."

"No way."

He waited for her to join him on the other side of the truck. Then he gripped her hand in his and led the way across the two lanes.

The van was about fifty yards below them, lying on the passenger side with two of its tires spinning.

Cash pulled out his cell. "I hope I can get a signal." He breathed a sigh of relief as he punched in 9-1-1.

A moment later, Jordan listened to him give the information and their location to someone on the other end. Everything had happened so fast. She was still trying to get her mind around it. By the time he slipped his cell back into his pocket, the van's tires had stopped spinning, most of the dust had settled, and she'd figured out what had happened.

Turning to him, she said, "You intended for him to go off the road, didn't you? That was your plan."

He met her eyes. "I won't deny that I was hoping it

would work out this way. That bastard was trying to kill you."

He half expected her to cringe or pull away, but she didn't. Instead, she wrapped her arms around him and pulled him close.

Cash couldn't have described the emotions that tumbled through him at the simple gesture. His knees nearly buckled. No woman had ever been able to push so many of his buttons so fast. She was taking him into uncharted territory. There was none of the fire or desperation he'd felt when they'd made love during the night or this morning. Now as he held her close to him, it was warmth that spread through him. And he felt suddenly and completely at home.

When she drew back, he didn't want to let her go.

"Thank you," she said simply.

Cash gathered his thoughts. "You helped, you know."

Her eyes narrowed. "How? You're the one who ought to start a new career as a race car driver."

He managed a smile. "You did everything I asked. You didn't ask useless questions, and you didn't fall apart."

She tilted her head to one side. "I don't usually fall apart. But I'm not sure you should depend on me not asking questions or being so obedient all the time."

He threw back his head and laughed. The sound was still lingering in the air when he pulled her close for a quick, hard kiss. At least his intention was to make it quick. But the softness of her lips, the flavors in her mouth tempted him to linger. Just for a moment. And that was all it took to have the heat igniting and spreading like a flash fire in a drought. Before he could think, he'd pulled her close and his hands were running over her, pressing, teasing, tormenting. It was as if his will had been snatched completely away.

It was the sudden feeling of helplessness that gave him the strength to pull back.

She was as breathless as he was, her eyes as surprised. "This is happening so fast."

"Can't argue with that." Another moment and he might have taken her right there where they stood. And he was damn sorry that he'd had to put on the brakes. Another time, another place he promised himself as he dropped his hands.

"You remember what you said about my not counting on you being so obedient all the time?"

She nodded.

"Why don't we give that a little test? What would you say if I asked you to stay here while I climbed down and checked on the driver?"

She shook her head firmly. "No way."

"See? One simple statement and you've totally adjusted my expectations."

Keeping her hand gripped in his, Cash led the way down to the wreck.

AN HOUR LATER, Jordan stood on the narrow shoulder of the drop-off giving her statement to Detective Shay Alvarez. He hadn't introduced himself, which made her suspect that Maddie knew him. How well was the big question. She'd made it her business to get his full name by the tried and true method of eavesdropping.

As Alvarez reviewed the notes he'd been taking, Jordan watched the scene below where a helicopter was lifting a stretcher carrying the injured body of the van's driver. For a moment, Alvarez also turned to watch until the man was safely pulled inside.

Earlier, when they'd reached the van, Cash had climbed up to the window and found the man still had a faint pulse.

They hadn't dared to move him. Not that they'd have been able to. The police had used some sort of a pulley to get the van upright before the medics could deal with getting him out.

The sun beat down ruthlessly, and the dusty breeze stirred up by the helicopter as it lifted brought even hotter air. Jordan felt sweat trickle down her back.

Detective Alvarez glanced down at his notebook. "You're sure you have no idea why this man tried to run you and Cash off the road?"

"No." That much was true, but she was beginning to feel little pangs of guilt because neither she nor Cash had admitted to him that she wasn't Maddie. That constituted lying to the police, didn't it?

"There have been some incidents of vandalism at the ranch," she said. "Someone tried to poison my horse, and this morning, my studio was vandalized."

Shay Alvarez took a moment to study her. "Cash told me."

Jordan figured that conversation must have taken place right after he'd arrived and taken Cash aside for a few moments. She'd gotten the distinct impression from their body language that they knew each other. But she could hardly ask. Maddie would know something like that.

After talking briefly to Cash and turning him over to one of the uniforms who'd accompanied him, Detective Shay Alvarez walked up to the curve that had ultimately sent the van out of control and examined the skid marks.

The man didn't look Hispanic. He was tall and lanky with broad shoulders and blue eyes. The moment he'd climbed out of his car he'd had her thinking of Matt Dillon from *Gunsmoke*.

Now as she met his penetrating gaze, she thought again of the sheriff in the old TV series. Matt Dillon had been one smart man, and she had a hunch that Shay Alvarez was, too. As the silence stretched between them, Jordan finally felt compelled to say something. Anything. "Do you know who the driver of the van is?"

"Not yet. He wasn't carrying any ID. Most professionals don't. But we may be able to trace him through his fingerprints."

"Do you think this incident might be related to the destruction of my studio?" Jordan asked.

In her peripheral vision, she could see Cash striding toward them. Relief surged through her. But it was short-lived.

"Perhaps. I might have a better idea about that if you'd tell me who you really are and why you're pretending to be Maddie Farrell?"

Cash reached them in time to hear the end of Shay Alvarez's question. With a grin he slapped the detective on the shoulder. "I was wondering if you'd figure it out."

"Were you going to tell me if I didn't?"

Cash shrugged. "Maybe."

Shay shook his head. "Knowing her identity is pretty crucial if you expect me to find out why the man in the van tried to kill her."

Cash's expression sobered. "I think he was trying to kill Maddie."

"Perhaps."

"When did you figure out she wasn't Maddie?"

Only then did Alvarez send him an answering smile. "It took me a bit. But she didn't seem to remember that I came out to the ranch when Brutus's hay was doctored."

Annoyance surged through Jordan. "Hey. I'm here and I don't appreciate being talked about as if I'm not."

"Yes, ma'am." The detective turned his charming smile on her and extended his hand. "I'm Shay Alvarez."

Jordan took the hand. "I'm Jordan Ware, Maddie's twin sister."

Shay's expression sobered. "Twins. That would explain the fact that you're a dead ringer for her. But why the impersonation?" He glanced at Cash again. "Or was that just a little joke on me?"

Cash shook his head. "Always so suspicious."

"The two of you have known each other for some time, I take it?" Jordan asked.

"Since high school," Shay said. "I didn't know Maddie had a twin."

"Neither did Maddie until a few days ago. Neither did I." Jordan explained her situation as concisely as she could.

"And I decided to pretend to be Maddie while I'm here because I want her jewelry show to be a success. I'm not sure her potential buyers would be as impressed if they discovered she'd skipped out on the show and they were left to do business with her twin."

"In that case, I won't rat you out," Shay promised. "But who else knows about the switch?"

"Only my mother's attorney, family members and the employees at Eva Ware Designs. Why?"

"Last night or this morning, Maddie's studio was broken into and destroyed. This morning you're nearly driven off the road. Clearly, the vandalism plaguing Maddie and her ranch has increased since you arrived in Santa Fe," Shay said. "And if someone is determined to break the will, getting rid of either you or your sister would work."

Jordan swallowed hard. "You think someone wants to kill Maddie or me because of my mother's will?"

He jerked his head in the direction of the wrecked van. "It's not the only explanation, but it does leap to mind. Money's always a powerful motivator."

"Jordan just found out this morning that her mother's hit-and-run death is being investigated as a possible homicide," Cash said.

Shay let out a low whistle. "You think there's a connection between that and this."

It wasn't a question, Jordan noted.

"I'm not a fan of coincidence, but as you say, it's not the only possibility," Cash said. "What do you know about Daniel Pearson?"

Shay's eyebrows shot up. "The real estate broker and wannabe mogul?"

Cash nodded.

"Mostly what I read in the society pages. He's well-connected socially, serves on a couple of museum and gallery boards, and he's using those connections to establish a thriving real estate business. Why?"

"Because for the last six months he's been pressuring Maddie to sell the ranch."

Shay thought for a minute. "I've met him a few times. He appears at all the events my mother bugs me to attend."

While Shay went on to describe Pearson as a social climber who thought he had a great deal of charm with the ladies, Jordan studied the two men standing in front of her.

Physically, they were similar. Both were tall and dark haired. Shay was a smoother dresser. His khaki slacks were neatly pressed. Cash's jeans were well-worn and fit like a second skin. Both radiated competence. In addition, the cowboy and the cop talked with the ease of old friends, their minds in tune, their respect for each other's ideas clear.

"You think Pearson is involved in this?" Shay asked.

"I think it's possible." Cash glanced up the road to the skid marks. "He could have hired the guy in the van. The same guy could have destroyed Maddie's studio last night and then waited around for us to go into Santa Fe. It was a good bet that she'd drive in today because of the big jewelry show tomorrow. And once Maddie's out of the picture, it's a pretty sure thing that the ranch will go on the market."

"Could be," Shay said. "But if he's been pressuring Maddie for six months, why all the urgency?"

"Perhaps he's under pressure, too," Jordan said. If Pearson is so anxious to list the ranch, he must have a buyer on the line."

Shay and Cash both turned to her.

"You've got a point," Shay agreed. "It's not enough for me to question Pearson. However, I could make some inquiries about who his buyer might be. My mother is on a couple of boards with Pearson's broker."

Cash smiled at him. "You do that."

"I assume you'll be sticking close to Ms. Ware."

Before Cash could reply, Jordan said, "I'm Maddie, remember?"

"Point taken." He took a step closer to her. "Cash won't tell you, but you were lucky to have him behind the wheel today. He knows every inch of this road."

"I know."

When a uniformed officer approached, Shay said, "Duty calls," and strode over to talk to the young man.

"You'll get back to us?" Cash called after him.

"Soon as I have something."

Turning, Cash took Jordan's hand. "Do you want to call it a day and go back to the ranch?"

She shook her head. "I want to go to Santa Fe. I came here to walk around in my sister's shoes, and I gave my word to Maddie that the jewelry show would go off without a hitch. I'm not letting anyone prevent me from doing either of those things."

He gripped her chin and brushed his mouth over hers. "I like your style, Jordan Ware."

7

CASH HANDED JORDAN a frozen cinnamon latte and set his coffee down on the table before he took the seat across from her.

She glanced up. "Thanks." Then she shifted her attention back to the notes Maddie had given her. It had been her idea to stop at the small restaurant across the street from the hotel where the jewelry show was scheduled to open on the following morning. She'd wanted a chance to prep herself in case she ran into anyone she should recognize.

He reached over to lay a hand on one of hers. "You'll do fine."

"I hope so." She linked her fingers with his. "There are a lot of people I'm going to have to keep straight. Some of them Maddie only sees at shows, but there are others she runs into more frequently."

"I might be able to help with some of them."

"Do you know Joe Manuelo?"

He thought for a moment. "We've never met, but I believe he's the man who cuts a lot of Maddie's stones."

"Yes. Maddie says he often visits the shows to see the end products of his work."

As she shifted her attention back to the notes, he studied their clasped hands. Hers was slender, delicate almost, a stark contrast to the woman he was coming to know. And he'd nearly lost his chance to know her better.

As Cash sipped his coffee, he glanced around the small outside patio. He'd taken less than three minutes to fetch their drinks, yet as he'd watched her sitting in the shade of a potted tree with the sunlight dappling over her, nerves had knotted tightly in his stomach. They'd had a close call.

And it didn't help that she was masquerading as Maddie. While he'd been waiting on their drinks, he'd considered pressing her to let him go forward with his idea of announcing their engagement. But there were problems with that plan. He was no longer sure it would be enough to protect her, and, more importantly, he no longer wanted to become engaged to Maddie. That was something he'd have to think about later.

The rational side of his mind told him that she was safe for now. After all, they were in the center of Santa Fe, and there would be some delay time before whoever had hired the thug in the van would learn that the mission had not been accomplished.

Unless the thug had an accomplice right here in Santa Fe. That might shorten their reprieve considerably.

They'll try again, nagged the tiny little voice at the back of his head. His gut instinct was to get Jordan as far away as he could. It was a sort of caveman response, and he couldn't recall ever having one with regard to a woman before.

But then he'd never responded to a woman the way he had to Jordan. He'd had some time while Shay had taken her statement to think about his reaction when he'd kissed her on the side of that road right after the accident. The strength and speed of his desire, the draining away of his willpower—both had been unprecedented. He was still baffled by it.

Even now as he watched her pouring over Maddie's notes, he wanted to reach out and touch her—just to run a finger down her cheek or tuck a strand of hair behind her ear. How long would it take him to erase that totally focused look from her face, he wondered. And how long could he wait to do it?

The current time and the place were all wrong, but that didn't stop his mind from conjuring up a fantasy. In it, they were alone. Not in Maddie's bedroom this time, but in his. It was only as he pictured it in his mind that he realized how much he wanted to see her in his home. She was standing in front of the fireplace dressed in nothing but those seductive scraps of lace and silk she'd been wearing the first night he'd seen her. The punch of heat was just as strong as it had been then—in spite of the fact that he knew what he'd find when he touched her and lowered her to the floor. Or he thought he knew. But every time he tasted her, wasn't there something new, some flavor that he hadn't discovered before…?

"Do you want more coffee?"

Her question snapped his mind back to reality and he silently cursed himself. "No." Quickly, he glanced around the patio. No one seemed to take notice of Jordan. No one seemed out of place.

But a pro would know how to blend in.

For a second, Cash toyed with the possibility of giving into his caveman urges and just carrying her off. And not merely because he wanted to be alone with her. Where could he take her so that she would be safe? To Albuquerque to a luxury hotel? His experience with the kinds of places Jordan must be used to were limited. Because of the ranch, his leisure time was always borrowed, and his idea of a great evening with a woman would be to spend it somewhere under the stars. He figured Jordan's fantasy would be a far cry from that.

She glanced up suddenly and there was curiosity in her eyes. "You're staring at me. It's distracting."

"Sorry. I like the view."

She took a sip of her latte. "Penny for your thoughts."

Cash decided to go with at least a partial truth. "I was wondering what your idea of a perfect romantic evening would be."

She blinked. "A perfect romantic evening? You're kidding, right?"

He felt heat rise in his neck. "No. I was thinking that I'd like to get you away from here where you'd be safe. Some place you'd enjoy. Some place where there'd be just the two of us. And I don't have a lot of experience with women like you."

Jordan set her drink down on the glass-topped table and folded her arms on its surface. "First of all, you're not going to get me away from here. Not for at least three weeks."

"Figured." He stopped himself before he could say more. He'd already dug a hole that might get deeper even without his help.

"Don't you get all overprotective on me."

He said nothing, and her eyes narrowed.

"Look, we're both smart, and we've been forewarned."

"Yeah. But I'm not a professional bodyguard. And you need one."

She waved that away with a little snort. "You've already saved my life once. Plus, anyone who can drive like you has good instincts. So do I. I thought we made a good team during the hair-raising ride down that hill."

"We did." And this wasn't the time for fantasy, he reminded himself.

"Then we'll handle this." She took another sip of her latte.

"I'm not leaving you alone—not even for a moment until we know who hired that thug."

She opened her mouth, shut it and then said, "Okay.

Okay. Now tell me what you meant by not having much experience with a woman like me?"

Cash held back an inner sigh. He'd known they'd get back to that, just as they'd gotten back to his fake engagement proposal. Once again, he went with the truth. "You're different for me, Jordan. It goes beyond the fact that I can't look at you without wanting you. There's something about you that's felt right for me from the beginning."

She swallowed. "We haven't really had a chance to talk about what's going on between us. Maybe we should. I've given it some thought. Not much." She traced one finger through the frost on her glass. "I have trouble thinking when you're around. But I did manage to decide something when I was in the shower. You're different for me, too. Having impromptu flings or affairs…" She paused to wave a hand. "I don't do that."

"Now there's something we have in common."

She drew in a deep breath. "But I want to make love with you again. I can't seem to keep myself from wanting that."

"Same goes for me."

"But that's about the end of the list of what we have in common."

"Oh, I don't know about that. We both love to ride. We both like ranches."

The corners of her mouth lifted, and the little line of worry faded from her forehead. "I like ranches in movies and books. But I'm sure fiction doesn't even crack the surface of what it's like to run a ranch, to live on one."

"You're thinking of your parents, of what you're beginning to suspect happened to them."

"They came from different worlds. And it didn't end happily for them. I'm not sure what we've begun here, but it can't last. We should both be honest about that. It would make things less complicated when I go back to New York."

He picked up her hand and raised it to his lips. "I'm not sure what we've begun yet, either. But why try to predict the ending? I'd rather see where it leads. Unless you're afraid."

Her chin lifted at that. "You don't scare me, cowboy."

"Good." He wished he could say that she didn't scare him, either. But she did. He was almost getting used to the jittery feeling in his stomach. Just as he was almost getting used to the fact that he couldn't be near her without experiencing that steady thrum of excitement in his blood. She felt it, too. He could see it in her eyes. They were darkening into the same deep shade of purple that coated the mountaintops as the sun dropped behind them. He took her hand. Maybe he couldn't carry her off to Albuquerque, but surely he could take her somewhere…

Then beyond her shoulder he caught a glimpse of Daniel Pearson approaching with a woman on his arm. Cash searched for the name and found it. Margo Lawson. Though he'd never formally met her, he'd seen her photo on Maddie's Web site, and Maddie had talked a lot about her. Margo owned one of the premiere boutiques in Santa Fe that showcased Maddie's jewelry.

"Don't look now but we're going to have company," he said to Jordan. "Daniel Pearson and one of the shop owners who carries Maddie's jewelry—Margo Lawson."

JORDAN IGNORED the nerves that danced briefly in her stomach. Her masquerade hadn't fooled Shay Alvarez. Would she be able to fool the two people who were approaching?

As if reading her thoughts, Cash squeezed her hand and whispered, "You'll be fine. You're a dead ringer for your sister. Just remember not to say too much. Maddie is quieter than you."

"Maddie?"

The male voice was still some distance away. Cash squeezed her hand and whispered, "Show time. Knock 'em dead."

"This is a pleasant surprise."

With a smile, Jordan rose from her chair and turned to study Daniel Pearson. He was medium height and handsome in an Ivy League, preppy kind of way. In the light suit, he looked every an inch a city boy, right down to the diamond winking on his pinky finger. "Daniel, it's good to see you."

Then she very nearly stiffened when the man hugged her and kissed her cheek. Maddie's notes hadn't mentioned they were that friendly. Or perhaps the man hugged all his potential clients?

Turning, Jordan smiled at the woman. "You, too, Margo. I was going to stop by the shop later this afternoon."

"You won't find me there," Margo drawled in a husky voice. "I'm taking the afternoon off to rest up for the big show tomorrow."

Jordan dredged up Maddie's notes. Margo was a tall brunette, who looked to be in her late thirties but was older. Her sundress was designer. Most importantly, she was Maddie's oldest client and supporter, so Jordan wanted very much to like her.

"I love the way you're wearing your hair." As Margo's eyes narrowed on her for a minute, Jordan felt her nerves dance again.

"It's a much more professional look than the braid. And it matches the sophisticated and feminine turn your latest designs have been taking. You should wear it that way to the show tomorrow."

Silently Jordan agreed, and she made a mental note to talk to her sister about a permanent change in her hairstyle.

Then Margo shifted her attention to Cash. "I hope you're going to introduce me to your friend."

"This is Cash Landry, my neighbor," Jordan said. She didn't like the way Margo was looking at Cash—as if she wanted a good-size taste of him.

"Margo Lawson," the brunette said as she took Cash's offered hand.

"Landry." Daniel sent him a nod, then turned to smile at Jordan. "This is delightful. I didn't expect to see you until the show tomorrow. You haven't forgotten that I'm taking you out to dinner afterward?"

Jordan thought fast. "I hope you don't mind if I bring Cash along. He's insisting on joining me in my booth at the show."

Annoyance flashed briefly into Daniel's eyes as he stepped closer to Jordan. "I'd planned on discussing business. You promised you'd have an answer for me about the ranch as soon as you put this show behind you."

Not about to let the grass grow under your feet, Jordan thought. As much as she might admire the move on a business level, she didn't like the fact that he was putting this kind of pressure on her sister.

Cash slipped a protective arm around Jordan's shoulders. "Someone broke into Maddie's studio this morning, and I plan on providing her with security until we find out who's responsible."

"Your new designs—did they steal them?" Margo's voice was laced with concern.

"No, thank heavens," Jordan said. "I keep them in a safe."

"They seemed more concerned with destroying the place than filling their pockets with jewelry or stones,"

Cash added. "I'll be staying at the ranch tonight and I'll drive her into Santa Fe for the show tomorrow."

Daniel was frowning now, but Jordan was pretty sure it wasn't the vandalism that was bothering him. She could read people well enough to know that he was a man who didn't like his plans changed. Trying to think how Maddie would handle the situation, she said, "Margo, why don't you join us for dinner tomorrow after the show and make it a foursome? That way you can amuse Cash while Daniel and I talk business?"

Margo kept her eyes on Cash. "I'd be delighted to amuse Cash. In fact, I'll look forward to it."

I'll just bet. There was no denying that it was jealousy she was feeling. But she could also feel Daniel Pearson relax.

"Great idea. Margo and I will see you tomorrow."

"Depend on it. I can't wait to see your latest collection."

With a brief nod to Cash, Daniel Pearson took Margo's arm and led her away down the sidewalk.

"I believe she's what they call a cougar," Cash murmured.

Jordan glanced at him and didn't like it a bit that he was still looking at Margo. "Cougar?"

His eyes when they met hers were brimming with laughter. "Isn't that what they call the older woman who's on the hunt for a younger man?"

"Cougar." She had to admit the term suited Margo Lawson. She had a feline grace and beneath it, Jordan sensed, a streak of ruthlessness. Plus, the woman hadn't done anything to hide the fact that she was interested in Cash. Jordan couldn't help being annoyed that she was still feeling jealous.

"And you're familiar with the term because you've had a lot of experience being 'hunted' by older women?"

He laughed and settled back into his chair. "You can

relax. I can handle Margo Lawson. I'm more worried about how you're going to handle Daniel Pearson."

With a frown, Jordan sat down. "*You* can relax on that score. Daniel Pearson's interest in Maddie isn't personal. He wants the ranch. And she has his number."

"Exactly." Cash's voice and eyes had turned hard. "But he thinks he's close to getting it."

Jordan's temper flared. "If you think Maddie's agreed to sell it to him, you're wrong. I'm positive she doesn't want to sell the place."

"It isn't a matter of what she wants. It may come down to necessity. And he seems pretty confident that he can close the deal." Cash fisted a hand on the table. "She's running fewer cattle, she's let all her hands go except for Mac McAuliffe. He hires on workers on a per diem basis when he needs them. I've been helping her out as much as I can. But your sister's proud. I don't know how much longer she'll continue to accept help from me. I *know* Maddie. She could very well let Pearson talk her into selling the ranch to make it easier on me."

Though she hadn't known her sister very long, Jordan found herself leaning toward his theory. "Not yet, she won't. Not for the next three weeks. Do you think that your prejudice against Daniel Pearson might be why you think he's behind the vandalism?"

Cash considered for a moment. "No. I believe he's a prime suspect. He knows she's in trouble, and a little vandalism here, a poisoned horse there, might be all it takes to have her signing on the dotted line."

Jordan thought for a minute. "If things are getting worse for Maddie, wouldn't he think it's just a matter of time before she agrees to let him sell the ranch? The look on his face when I said you'd be coming with me to dinner told me he had very high expectations for tomorrow night.

He thinks his plans are right on track. It doesn't mesh with hiring someone to kill her. Plus, he didn't look at all surprised to see me here."

"Perhaps it's Pearson's buyer who's getting desperate," Cash said. "He or she could be acting on their own."

"Why?" The question hung in the air between them for a few beats. Jordan tapped her fingers on the table. "Maddie's having trouble making ends meet, so why is someone so anxious to get their hands on the ranch?"

"Perhaps Shay's theory is correct and the attempt on your life is somehow connected to your mother's will?"

"Maybe. Could be I'm prejudiced against that idea because it would mean that someone in my family could be involved. And I just don't see it. Maybe I don't want to see it. In any case, I'm more anxious than ever to take that tour of the ranch you promised me."

Cash's brows shot up. "You think you'll find the answer there?"

"Maybe. Maddie's an artist. She's like my mother. I'm a business person. I see things from a very different angle. I wonder if my father were here—if he'd known what was going on—if he'd know what to do."

His smile was slow and easy. "I know one thing for sure. Mike Farrell would have liked you, Jordan Ware." Then he took her hand and drew her to her feet. "Why don't we go turn that expert businessperson's eye on Maddie's booth?"

CHAOS. That's what Jordan saw when she stepped into the hotel's cavernous exhibition room. Her first impression was that a huge movie set was being constructed. Saws buzzed and screeched through plywood. Carts rattled as they carried display cases, tables and chairs across the space. The smell of paint and woods chips mingled with the scent of flowers that were being placed around pillars and doorways.

Beside her, Cash was taking in the room as carefully as she was. She bet his mind was on the bodyguard thing. But right now, she had to concentrate on her job, which was to represent Maddie as well as she could.

From what she could make out, booths would eventually line the walls and run in several rows down the center of the room. That coincided with what she was used to. Thank heavens she'd had some experience with jewelry shows. Her mother had occasionally showcased her designs at the Jacob Javits Center in New York.

"My mother always hated these shows," she said.

"Maddie doesn't care for them much, either. She doesn't like the sales end of the business."

"It's an essential part. Without it, the pieces run the risk of spending their lives in display cases. My mother's jewelry is meant to be worn. Maddie's is, too. I'm coming to believe that two of them are a lot alike. It's such a shame that they never got to know each other."

For a moment Jordan felt a mix of emotions swamp her—regret, anger, frustration. Once again, her mind turned to the question of why her parents had cut themselves off from one of their daughters.

"It is a shame." Cash reached for her hand and gave it a squeeze. "You should have had the chance to know your father, too. At least, you'll get to know him a little better once you settle in at the ranch."

Jordan pushed the flood of feelings away. These were things she'd think about later, deal with later. It helped that Cash was there, and that he held her hand.

Turning, she studied him for a moment, absorbing once more the strong, lean face that her hands had explored so thoroughly before she'd even seen him. And she remembered the pleasure that came from merely touching him. Not just his face, but that long, hard body.

As if he sensed the direction her thoughts had taken, he turned to her, and the heat in his eyes had her breath stopping in her throat. Suddenly, they might have been alone in the room. Workmen stepped around them, voices chattered, saws buzzed, but to Jordan, the sounds came from a distance. All she could think, all she knew was that she wanted Cash to kiss her. All she felt was a pull that came not just from him, but from something edgy and needy inside of her.

All she had to do was move just a little closer and his mouth would cover hers. She would feel again that sharp, dazzling pleasure she'd felt when he'd kissed her on the side of the road. She took the step.

"If I kiss you, I might not be able to stop." His voice was low and rough. "Do you want me to see if I can get us a room?"

For a moment, Jordan was outrageously tempted. To spend the rest of the afternoon in a hotel room with Cash. To think only about the pleasure that they could bring one another. It would be wild and wonderful.

And completely impossible. Her sister was depending on her. "I can't."

Cash squeezed her hand and then released it. "Later, then. That's a promise, Jordan."

Her hand trembled as she took a catalog from a box. But scanning through it helped her gather her thoughts. "I want to see where they've put Maddie."

The catalog listed the names and photos of exhibitors, along with a booth number. And in another moment or so, she'd be able to focus on them. The pictures would help tomorrow, she thought. She was banking on the fact that buyers would introduce themselves to her or hand her a card. But over the years, Maddie had become acquainted with other designers, and the last thing Jordan wanted to do was snub them. Of course, Maddie had named and described them, but having a picture—well, it truly was worth a thousand words. Noting Maddie's booth number, she located it on the floor map of the exhibition hall and led the way.

"It's a good spot," she said when they reached it, pleased that her legs were working and her thoughts almost refocused. "Most people will take at least one complete tour of the room, but sometimes they skip the rows that run in the center."

She watched as the workmen—one white-haired with a grizzled beard and a muscular build, the other just barely out of his teens, unloaded a stainless-steel-and-glass case. She could see from a glance at adjacent spaces that each exhibitor was getting one. When the display case was centered in the space, she approached the older man and extended her hand.

"Hi, I'm Maddie Farrell. This will be my booth tomorrow. I'm supposed to be getting two display cases."

The white-haired man immediately frowned. "Not according to what I got here." He pulled a clipboard off his cart, flipped over a few pages, then angled it so she could see. "Booth one-twelve—one case."

As Jordan sighed and turned to Cash, she met his eyes and hoped that he would follow her lead. "It's Aunt Amy again. She assured me she'd arranged for the extra case. I asked her several times. I'm afraid she's getting more and more forgetful…"

Cash placed his hand on her shoulder. "You're going to have to think about letting her go."

"I'm not sure that I can. I'm the only family she has left, and she's worked all her life. I can't imagine her sitting home and taking up knitting." Then with an apologetic smile, she turned back to the man with the clipboard. "My aunt—who is my secretary—said she'd talked to the man in charge of the exhibits and arranged for me to have a second case. Is there any chance that you could hunt me up one? I know you're busy."

"Busy doesn't even begin to describe it, lady." But his frown was fading. "How old is your aunt?"

"Nearly eighty."

He studied her for a moment, then nodded. "You keep her on. My grandson and I will hunt you up a second case if we can."

Jordan beamed a smile at him. "Thank you so much."

"Nice job," Cash said in an undertone as the two men wheeled their cart away.

"Thanks for picking up on what I was trying to do."

"My pleasure."

She was about to turn back to the case when she spotted a pretty young woman in tribal Navajo dress hurrying toward her. Even as her mind raced, her stomach knotted.

"It's Lea Dashee," Cash murmured in a low tone.

Right. Lea Dashee had gone to college with Maddie. She was slender, with long black hair, and the white dress she wore, with its silver beading, looked stunning on her. Silver jewelry design had been a tradition with the women in Lea's family for hundreds of years.

"She's Pete Blackthorn's granddaughter. He's the turquoise prospector I told you about. She may know how we can contact him."

As Lea reached them, Jordan smiled. "Hello."

The young woman threw her arms around Jordan and gave her a hard hug. "So good to see you. It's a shame that we only get to see each other a couple of times a year at one of these things."

"Don't we say that all the time?"

"We do." Lea laughed. "But then we go back and bury ourselves in our studios." She drew back and gave Jordan a swift study. "Beautiful as always."

"Ditto."

Lea laughed again. "We always say that, too. And tomorrow we'll oooh and aaah over each other's designs." She took one of Jordan's hands and squeezed it. "You bring your appointment calendar with you. We're going to make a definite date. Have lunch and hit some galleries. I'm going to watch you write it in."

"It's a deal." Jordan made a mental note to hunt up an appointment calendar. It wouldn't do for her to use her BlackBerry.

Lea turned her attention to Cash. "Don't tell me you've suddenly developed an interest in jewelry?"

Cash tilted his head in Maddie's direction. "She dragged me here in case she needed some hauling and lifting."

"Good idea! I may ask a favor if you're coming back tomorrow?"

Cash nodded. "Sure thing. But I need a favor right now. Maddie's trying to get in touch with your grandfather. Do you know where we might find him?"

Lea thought for a minute. "He hasn't been back to his trailer for a few days. Usually when he camps out, it's in the hills to the southeast of Maddie's ranch." She glanced back at Jordan. "I'll bet if you take a ride out, you'll run into him there."

"Thanks," Jordan said.

Lea waved a hand as she hurried away. "Tomorrow."

Jordan turned to Cash. "I don't know what I'd do without you."

"My pleasure." And it was, Cash thought. His pleasure deepened as he watched her move closer to examine the beveled glass case in great detail. She was totally focused now, just as she had been at the small café when she'd been poring over Maddie's notes.

"If they get me that second case, we'll angle them into

a V." Then she circled to the back of the booth and studied the wall. It had been painted a sunny yellow.

"Not bad. The color should work with the turquoise. And I packed some swatches of silk in nearly the same color."

As she turned back to the display case, the wall behind her suddenly began to tilt forward. Moving on instinct, Cash shoved Jordan aside and braced both his palms against it.

For several seconds he struggled unsuccessfully against the downward momentum of the wall. He heard an ominous creak as the base slid an inch backward and the pressure against his arms built.

"Cash?"

"Stay away." Sweat beaded on his forehead. Fear arrowed through him. He wasn't going to win this battle.

8

TWO SETS OF HANDS suddenly joined Cash's on the wall of the booth. Working as a team, he and the two men who'd come to his aid managed to get it back into position. The moment it was upright and balanced, Cash turned to one of the workmen. "Thanks. What the hell happened?"

One of the men had already moved behind the wall and dropped to his knees. Cash joined him.

"Looks like someone didn't fasten the braces tight enough. Pretty careless. These things can do quite a bit of damage if they fall."

"Thanks." Cash noted that there was plenty of room for someone to fit behind the booth. Plus there was an exit doorway right behind the wall. He shoved through it, but the hallway was empty.

"There. That should hold it," said the man.

"Thanks." Cash stepped around the now secured wall and moved to Jordan's side. Pitching his voice low, he said, "Someone may have purposely unloosened the braces and then slipped out of the room."

Or perhaps they'd edged their way behind several of the other booths and joined the throng of people in the exhibition hall. He scanned the room. Everyone was busy. Carts were moving, workmen were hoisting walls. Hammers pounded, saws whirred. No one seemed out of place. Not one person glanced guiltily in their direction. And no one was making a beeline for the door. Frustration raged inside of him. He wanted badly to get his hands on someone.

"You think someone wanted that wall to fall on purpose?" Jordan asked.

She had turned to study it. He followed the direction of her gaze, and in his mind he pictured just how the wall might have fallen, trapping her against the display case on the floor. The glass would have shattered, and she could have been badly hurt. "I'm not willing to completely trust coincidence."

"But who would have known we're here?"

"Good question." And he didn't like the answers. "Pearson and your friend Margo knew we were headed for the exhibition room."

"But if something happens to me, Daniel won't get to list the ranch. He seemed very focused on talking me into that tomorrow night at dinner."

"Perhaps he only wanted to injure you, make you vulnerable to his offer." Cash ran a hand through his hair even as his gaze raked the room again. "Or maybe I'm getting paranoid." He met her eyes. "Do you have everything you need for now?"

"Yes."

"C'mon." Cash urged her toward the door. He wanted to get her someplace safe.

Jordan's cell rang the moment they stepped out of the exhibition room. Even as she pulled it out of her pocket, Cash nudged her against a wall between two potted plants. From their position, he could keep his eye on the lobby and the main door to the exhibition room.

"Maddie? What is it?"

Cash heard the fear in Jordan's voice. Neither had

expected Maddie to call again. It couldn't be good news. Moving closer, he leaned down, and Jordan tipped her cell so he could hear.

JORDAN SAT in the pickup next to Cash as they drove back to the ranch. Her head was still spinning from the news that Maddie and Jase had given them.

A professional hit woman had tried to shoot Maddie in Central Park.

Just thinking about it had fear tightening in her stomach. She'd nearly lost her sister.

When Cash had reported what they'd learned to Shay Alvarez and related what had happened at the exhibition hall, the detective suggested that they return to the ranch and provided them with a police escort home. The two men in the cruiser following them would stay, keep the ranch under surveillance and escort them back into Santa Fe for the jewelry show in the morning.

As they started up the hill where they'd nearly been driven off, Cash said, "You're too quiet. You have to be worried about Maddie. Talk to me."

She turned to study him. In profile, he looked tough and rugged. And he was. But he also had a streak of kindness that ran bone-deep.

"I can't seem to get my mind around it." She swallowed hard. "Someone tried to shoot my sister."

He flicked her a glance. "Someone tried to kill you, too, Jordan."

"I know. It's hard enough to accept that, but when I think of Maddie being in the sights of a professional sniper…I might never have gotten a chance to know her. And what if it happens again? What if the next shot hits its target?"

Now that she'd started talking, Jordan couldn't seem to

stop. "That's why I didn't tell her about the man trying to drive us off the road. I didn't want her to feel helpless and angry. More than anything, I want to go to her. I want us both to go to New York and help protect her. But because of the will, we can't. And we don't have a clue about who's behind all of this."

She could hear the rising hysteria in her voice, so she clamped her mouth shut.

"I think you were right not to tell her. Jase and she need to focus all their energy on figuring out who's trying to kill her. But it may be the same person who's trying to kill you."

Jordan stared at him. "You think?"

"Two professionals hired to take out two sisters on the same day?" Cash's tone was dry. "It's hard to think there isn't a connection."

He was right. She knew that. But she just hadn't wanted to think about it. A wave of disgust moved through her. "I'm being a coward."

Cash snorted. "A coward? You wouldn't know how to be one."

"Ever since the phone call, I've been wallowing in fear and self-pity. I don't do that. I deal with things."

He glanced at her again. "You don't have to deal with this alone, Jordan. And Maddie doesn't, either. Your friend Jase owns a security firm. He's got men he can call on for backup. And according to Maddie, he was the one who saved her life in Central Park."

His voice was as calm, as if he were trying to settle a skittish horse, but Jordan could see the tension in his jaw. When he reached over to cover her hand with his, she felt it in the tightness of his grip.

"You're worried that you don't have enough backup to protect me."

"Yeah. I'm worried. I'll feel better when Jase's brother, D.C., gets here," he said.

That was the one thing that Jase had insisted on—sending his brother to Santa Fe—and Cash hadn't objected.

"Have you ever met him?"

"Yes, back in the days when Jase and I were in college. He's a year younger than Jase and he went into the army right after he graduated. I didn't even know he was in New York."

"What's he like?"

"Jase used to tell me stories about the trouble they'd gotten into as kids. He claimed that D.C. was the brains behind most of their escapades. Even in college, he had a reputation for being a bit on the wild side. But I imagine a couple of tours of duty in Iraq have settled him down."

"He's in the military police, right?"

"Yes."

Cash glanced at his watch. "He's going to call when he lands in Santa Fe, but I don't imagine that will be until late tonight or early tomorrow morning."

Jordan turned to study him. "You worry too much. I'm used to taking care of myself."

"I'm beginning to understand that. I'm wondering why."

She could have given him an evasive answer. But he was always so forthright with her. "My mother was always focused on her jewelry design business, so I grew up trying to take care of the practical stuff. When I discovered early on that I didn't have her creative flair for jewelry design, I went to business school. I figured I could make my contribution that way."

"Your contribution to what?"

"Her dream."

"What about your dreams? Do you ever do anything just for Jordan?"

"Of course."

But when he said nothing more, she started to think. She'd done things for herself. She'd wanted to get her business degree. For as long as she could remember, she'd wanted to make a contribution to Eva Ware Designs. But had she ever done anything *only* for herself? Once more she turned to study Cash. Immediately, she felt the tingle of awareness, the heat of anticipation that he could ignite in her by simply being there. She wanted to touch him. And more.

"In your whole life, what have you done exclusively for yourself?" he asked.

"You. You're what I'm doing for me." She hadn't expected him—wasn't sure she was even ready for him. But if she hadn't ended up with him in Maddie's bed…if she'd had to go through life not knowing him, not knowing what they could bring to each other…she didn't even want to think about that.

"I have to confess I don't understand what's happening between us, but I'm sitting here right now wondering what would happen if I touched you."

He shot her a slow smile. "If that police cruiser weren't right on our tail, I could come up with a few ideas of exactly what we could do if you touched me. Have you ever made love in the back of a pickup?"

"No." But she was already starting to imagine what it might be like.

"We'll have to put it on our to-do list. Once we get back to the ranch, what do you have to do to get ready for the show tomorrow?"

"I want to take Maddie's jewelry out of the safe and experiment with some ways to display it. Then I'll review her notes again on the various buyers who might drop by.

There are also a couple of designers she's friends with besides Lea. Luckily I can look them up in the catalog and match names with photos."

He shot her a smile. "Sounds like a pretty full agenda. Before you dig in, why don't we take the horses out for a ride?"

The idea delighted her. "You mean it?"

"I don't say things I don't mean. I think we both need a break. It should be safe enough. It would be pretty tough for anyone to follow us—unless they were on horseback, too."

A careful man, she thought. And something inside of her warmed. She really wasn't used to someone looking out for her. Of course, Jase cared about her, but she'd never thought of him as her...what? Protector?

"We'll ride in the direction of the hills east of the ranch. There's a canyon there I want to show you. And it has the added attraction of being a place where Pete Blackthorn does a lot of his prospecting."

"Two birds with one stone?"

He shot her a grin. "Busted."

It occurred to her that the more she got to know Cash, the more she liked him. And she had a strong hunch that it was going to complicate their relationship. Big-time. He might not like to predict endings, but she did. So she couldn't let herself forget that whatever they discovered together would end in three weeks. But maybe they could enjoy each other and part as friends.

Something tightened around her heart. Perhaps if her parents had foreseen the inevitable ending, they wouldn't have been forced into difficult decisions.

AIR AS DRY as the land beneath them whipped past as they rode toward the hills jutting upward behind the ranch.

Once they'd exited the corral, they'd let the horses set the pace. Cash had chosen Lucifer, a black stallion he'd said had belonged to her father, and she was on Maddie's Brutus. Both horses were eager for a fast run, and they galloped side by side.

The only sound to mar the silence was the pounding of hooves. The hat she'd worn to shield her from the sun lay forgotten on the back of her neck as Jordan let her body familiarize itself with the movements of the horse beneath her. Gradually, her mind emptied.

Riding was something she loved. It had become an integral part of her life. Sports had never been her thing, and though her mother loved working out in a gym, Jordan just didn't see the point.

She'd made it a habit to get away at least twice a month to ride Julius Caesar, the horse she kept just north of the city. For her, the time she spent riding was better than going to a spa. It cleared her mind, toned her body and often provided her with a fresh perspective on some challenge she faced at work.

She spotted the fence coming up in the distance.

"You game?" Cash asked.

"You bet." She bent low over Brutus, using the stirrups to raise herself slightly as the horses sailed over in unison. She laughed and urged him on.

Usually, riding emptied her mind. But Cash kept sneaking in. Earlier, when they'd gotten back to the ranch, they'd showered separately as they had in the morning. Jordan had thought about joining Cash in the other bathroom, but her practical side had won out. If they indulged in shower games, they wouldn't have as much time for their ride. And after all, they'd have to shower again when they returned to the ranch…

While she'd selected clothes from Maddie's closet, she'd

heard Cash puttering in the kitchen. When she'd joined him, she found he'd filled canteens with water and packed them an early dinner in a saddlebag. The man thought ahead.

That's what she should be doing, too—thinking of Maddie's jewelry and playing some arrangements through her mind. But with the wind in her hair and the breathtaking scenery around her, she simply couldn't. Giving in to the moment, she simply let herself enjoy.

A short time later, they reached the spiky patches of grass at the foot of the hills and reined to a stop.

"Thank you," she said. "I needed that."

"Me, too. If you turn, you can get a different view of the ranch," Cash added.

Jordan glanced over her shoulder, then urged her horse around. The sun was lowering in the sky in front of those huge picture windows, and the back of the buildings were throwing off shadows. From this distance, the ranch, the stable, the bunkhouse and the white fences of the corrals all looked like a child's play set.

A memory flickered at the edge of her mind, and this time it pushed through. What she saw in front of her reminded her again of that toy ranch set that Santa had brought her all those years ago. Shifting the reins to one hand, she pressed fingers against her temple.

"What is it?" Cash asked.

"I had a toy ranch when I was small. There were buildings, fences that pulled apart, horses and cattle. I used to spend hours moving everything into different configurations. I thought about it earlier, but it didn't click."

She turned to him. "Maybe that's why I feel—I have felt from the moment I arrived—that I've come home. I thought maybe it was because I had some memory of this place. But that's ridiculous."

"Why? You have proof based on your birth certificates

that you and Maddie were both born here. This probably *was* your first home."

"But I was so little. How could I possibly remember?"

"Children remember love. I can tell you one thing. Your father—Mike Farrell—loved you. I saw the way he was with Maddie. He adored her. He taught her to ride. And when she showed an interest in jewelry design, he converted that building into a studio for her."

"He converted it? I assumed he built it for Maddie as a studio."

"No, it's been there as long as I can remember. When she was younger, it was her playhouse." He winced. "One time she asked me to come in and play with her dolls."

Jordan grinned. "Did you?"

"*Dolls?* Not on your life. I saved myself by persuading her to enjoy more manly things. I taught her how to rope a cow. Play poker. I'm probably personally responsible for turning her into a tomboy. Before she went to college, I even taught her some karate moves."

"Karate moves?"

"Just some basic stuff. They offered some classes in our high school, and Shay and I signed up for them. Maddie wanted to be able to defend herself. She's pretty good."

"Yes, she is." Jordan remembered the way Maddie had handled Adam right after the reading of the will. "I think I'm just beginning to know my sister." And that reminded her that she'd very nearly lost her sister.

Cash took her chin in his hand and turned her face toward his. "We're not going to think about Maddie's near miss right now. We're on a break, remember?"

"Okay."

"What you should know is that your sister was one of the most important things in Mike's life. He couldn't possibly have felt differently about a second daughter."

Jordan thought of the framed photo she'd discovered of Maddie sitting on Brutus and her father standing next to her. The love had been palpable.

"Then why…?"

"Why did they separate you? You may never find the answer to that."

"I know. I know."

"C'mon, I have something else to show you."

They eased the horses into a walk. Ahead of them, she saw a sharp break in the hills, and Cash turned into it. To her surprise, they were suddenly in a narrow canyon with the sheer sides of a cliff rising on either side. The ground beneath the horses' hooves was rough and rutted, and the trail twisted and turned through the mountain.

When a fork appeared, Cash led the way to the right. Before long, the trail opened into a small clearing. At one end, surrounded by tumbled rocks was a pond. The horses, sensing water, moved quickly toward it. As he dismounted and took the reins of both animals, Cash kept his eyes on Jordan's face. She knew how to guard her feelings when the occasion demanded. He'd seen her mask fear on that wild ride down the mountain. And she'd done a good job of hiding her nerves when she'd met Daniel Pearson and Margo Lawson.

But she wasn't doing that now. He saw surprise, wonder and pleasure race across her features. And he decided he'd made the right choice.

"It's like an oasis," she said.

"Your sister and your father called it paradise."

When she'd dismounted, he led the two horses closer to the edge of the water and let them drink. Thanks to the height of the cliffs surrounding them, the pond was half in shadow, and a cool breeze moved across the water.

Her eyes shifted to the cliffs, and there were still traces of awe on her face. "How?"

"Some kind of underground spring feeds it. Water is rare in these parts, so Mike Farrell kept this a well-guarded secret."

She glanced at him. "But he shared it with your family?"

"*After* I discovered it. The canyon is a shortcut between the two ranches. When I told him about it, Mike swore me to secrecy. He came from a long line of ranchers and he was very protective of his land. He didn't want to do anything to encourage tourists trespassing or to exploit the land that he'd inherited in a commercial way. He wanted very much to pass on his heritage the way it was handed down to him. My father was a lot like him. They were 'green' before they even invented the name for it."

"Then it's very important that Maddie hang on to the ranch—so that she can pass it down."

"Yes."

"If she's losing money, then I need to come up with a business plan that will allow her to start making some profit. Three weeks from now, if everything goes well, she'll have the money from my mother's will to invest. Of course, she'll sink some of it into her design business. But she'll also have enough to invest in the ranch. The problem will be not to throw good money after bad."

"What are you thinking of, Jordan?"

"You'll think I'm crazy. But it's one of the things I used to pretend when I was so fascinated playing with my ranch toy. I mean, what did I know about cattle ranching?"

"What did you pretend?"

"That I was operating a dude ranch. What else would a Yankee tenderfoot come up with? But why couldn't Maddie do both? She could protect her heritage, still keep it a running ranch, but open up a new business. She could add on to the bunkhouse or even build a new structure just beyond the stables to house guests. Offer comfortable accommodations, gourmet food, and give them a chance to get into the cowboy thing."

"Whoa. The cowboy thing?"

She waved a hand. "You'll have to help me with that. But I was thinking to start out very exclusive at first, offer guests the chance to really participate in ranch life, rounding up cattle, fixing fences. Just a ride through that canyon would be exciting. It's like a movie set."

Cash let her talk until she ran down. He led the horses over to a patch of grass and loosely fastened the reins to a tall shrub. Then he lifted off the saddlebag and the two canteens. When he walked back to her, she was still staring across the pond, seeing something that he didn't.

"I hate to rain on your parade, but how is Maddie going to run a dude ranch and still grow her design business?"

She turned to him. "Yes, that's the kicker, isn't it? Do you see anything wrong with the dude ranch idea besides that?"

"No. There are other dude ranches in the area, but you've got some unique ideas in terms of serving gourmet food and creating the 'cowboy' experience." Setting the saddlebag down, he took out two glasses and a bottle of wine. "I brought red because I figured white would be too warm."

She studied him for a moment. "You don't seem like the kind of man who'd be into wine."

"Your father got me interested in it. He has a good cellar."

She waited until he'd uncorked the bottle, handed her a glass and tipped wine into it. "You're not sounding very enthused about my idea."

"I'm thinking about it."

When he'd filled his own glass, she clicked hers against it before she sipped.

"Maddie has a lot on her plate right now, and she's very intent on her business. When she's in that studio, she loses track of everything. It's one of the reasons the ranch is suffering. When Mike was alive, he'd drag her out and insist she do other things. If I didn't come over and talk her into going riding or into a game of poker, I'm not sure she'd ever come out."

"Wow." Jordan found a flat rock and sat down. "She sounds exactly like my mother. I insisted that she and I have lunch together every Wednesday, and then we'd go to a matinee or shopping or to a gallery. I always had it planned out very carefully. Otherwise, she never would have taken a break."

For a moment, she sat in silence. Cash moved to sit on a rock facing hers. She'd turned away to stare out over the water again, and he could tell her mind was still focused entirely on the idea of a dude ranch. She wasn't a lot different than her mother and sister once she got her teeth into a business idea.

It was time to distract her. She'd taken the hairpiece off when she'd showered, and the wind had given a good toss to her hair. He reached out and touched just the ends.

She immediately turned to him. "I appreciate it that you're worried about Maddie. But I'm going to figure out a way. That's what a good business plan is for. And I won't hurt my sister. You can trust me on that."

He took the hand that wasn't holding the wineglass and raised it to his lips. "I do."

"Good." He released her hand and leaned back enough to stretch out his legs and cross them. He wanted very badly to touch her again. But not yet.

"Thanks for bringing me here. It's a good thinking place."

"I didn't bring you here just so you could think, Jordan."

"You wanted to share the beauty of the place."

"Partly. But I had another reason, too."

"What?"

"I brought you here to seduce you."

Jordan felt her throat go dry as dust. She sipped her wine. "You don't have to. I just have to look at you to want you." It was the simple, somewhat terrifying truth.

"I was considering earlier where I might bring you. Someplace private and safe where we could take our time. We haven't taken a lot of time."

"No." He hadn't made a move. All he'd done was sit there and talk to her in that slow, quiet drawl. But his eyes held such heat, such promise, that some of her wine spilled over the side of the glass. When she set it down carefully on the ground, she saw that her hand was trembling.

Seduction, she thought. It might not be such a bad idea. Rising, she sent him a smile. Then she lifted her hat off and tossed it on the rock behind her. Keeping her gaze locked on his, she toed her boots off next. Her knowledge of strippers was limited to the musical *Gypsy,* and it had been years since her mother had taken her to see it on Broadway. But if her memory served her, they always started with peripherals—gloves, hats, shoes.

She watched him as she undid her belt buckle. He hadn't moved. He was still sitting on the rock, his long legs stretched out in front and crossed at the ankles. On the surface, he appeared relaxed. The way his fingers gripped the wineglass told her he wasn't. He might speak slowly and move slowly, but there was always that energy she sensed below the surface. He kept it on a tight leash, and she wondered just what she could do to release it.

She took the belt off slowly. Since the buckle was one

of Maddie's, she rolled the leather around it for protection before she set it on the ground.

Still smiling, she slipped her fingers beneath her T-shirt, pulled it off and tossed it behind her.

"What are you doing, Jordan?"

Her brows rose at that. "I'm just getting into this seduction thing. Don't you like it?"

His gaze dropped to the lacy bra that still covered her breasts.

"Yeah, I do like it. A lot. But my idea was to seduce *you*."

"You still can. Later." She pulled open the snap of her jeans. In the silence, the sound was erotic. The horses stirred. So did something deep inside of her. Cash set his glass down and didn't notice when it tipped over.

Power pumped through her followed by arousal as she slowly lowered her zipper. She wanted to go to him then and drag off his clothes. Instead, she hooked her thumbs in the waistband of her jeans and slid them slowly down over her hips. When they dropped to the ground, she stepped out of them and sent him another smile. "Okay. Your turn."

9

HIS TURN? She was standing there in the sunlight, dressed in nothing but two wisps of lace that had been designed to make a man beg. With his body burning and his head spinning, Cash knew exactly how he wanted to take his turn. All of the time she'd been slipping out of her clothes, he'd been weaving a fantasy in his mind.

Three strides and he could turn her around, bend her over that rock she'd been sitting on. It would take only seconds to get rid of the barriers between them—his jeans and that froth of lace she was wearing. And he could be inside of her. Cash felt his mind spin, his thoughts blur. The pounding ride would be wild, wonderful—and it would relieve the aching desire she'd ignited inside of him.

Cash reined in his thoughts. It wasn't his plan to take her against a rock. Plus, he wasn't at all sure that if he stood up, his legs would support him.

But two could play at the game she'd just started. He'd never stripped for a woman before. But he knew how to take off his clothes. Focusing his attention on the job at hand, he took off his boots. Still seated, he met her eyes and smiled.

"More," she said.

"You got it."

His eyes never left hers as he pulled his shirt out of his jeans and then began work on the buttons.

"I could help with that," she said.

"I can handle it. Besides, turnabout's fair play, don't you think?"

"I can only think about wanting you. Now."

It occurred to Cash that she had a better handle on this seduction thing than he had. But he was a quick learner. Once he'd tossed the shirt aside, he had no choice but to stand up and test his legs. They held. The jeans came next. He had to bend over to free his feet. When he straightened, she was smiling at him, one arm outstretched, her finger crooked. Oh yeah, she definitely had an advantage in the seduction game.

"I want you. Now."

"Ditto." He moved quickly then. But when he reached her, he didn't turn her and bend her over the rock as he'd fantasized doing. Instead, he swept her into his arms and covered her mouth with his.

Then holding her close, he turned and leaped into the pond.

When Jordan surfaced, she was still locked in Cash's arms. Her mouth was still fused with his. And the fire that the kiss had ignited in her body more than blocked out the coolness of the water. When he pulled away, she nearly cried out in protest.

"Breathe," he said.

"Okay." Since she could feel her lungs burn when she did, it was good advice. She met his eyes. "I didn't see that coming."

"It was a last-minute decision, one of several alternatives I had in mind. I wanted to slow things down a bit."

"And you thought a little dip would do the trick?" She shifted suddenly, snaking her arms and legs around him, then wiggling down his body until the hard length of him was pressed against her just where she wanted him. Holding tight, she moved up and down his penis. Fire shot through her again, and she was almost certain she saw steam rise from the surface of the pond. "What do you want now?"

"You know what I want." Gripping her buttocks, Cash lifted her up so that her legs were around his waist.

She struggled for position, but his hands allowed no movement.

"You have some very dangerous moves." His voice was raw.

"My pleasure."

To her surprise, he chuckled and then rested his head for a moment against her forehead. "How about a truce? I want to take my time with you, Jordan. We've been on a real fast track—no detours. Let me try this my way."

She drew back, looked into his eyes. And she would have agreed to anything he wanted. "Okay."

He touched his mouth to hers, and though his impulse was to devour, he didn't. Instead, he used his tongue to trace the outline of her lips. Then he toyed with them— nibbling at the corners, nipping on her bottom lip.

Slipping his hands into her hair, he held her in place as he kissed her, slowly, thoroughly. There were flavors here he'd never lingered over. First he feasted on the initial tartness, then that incredible sweetness. It reminded him of the homemade lemonade his mother had fixed for him when he was a child. Addictive. He'd never been able to stop drinking it until the glass had been drained.

When he felt her body go lax and her legs slipped away from his waist, a simmering heat shot straight to his center. But he banked it down as he took his mouth on a lazy journey over her face, reacquainting himself with every angle and curve. Her breath caught and released, caught and released. Each time it did, his own pulse quickened.

Using his tongue, he traced her ear and whispered, "So far, what do you think?"

"I can't…I just…want…"

Cash drew back then and looked into her eyes. Confusion, need and arousal made an incredible aphrodisiac. But he didn't want to end it yet. When her head dropped back, he cupped it in one hand and began to explore her neck and shoulders. Even beneath the sheen of water, he could smell her scent, an exotic fragrance he suspected wasn't a perfume. It was subtle at her throat, stronger as he made his way to the valley between her breasts. She still wore the lacy bra, but through the sheer material he saw her nipple. When he closed his mouth over it and used teeth and tongue, she spoke his name in a strangled gasp.

There was so much heat, Jordan didn't think she could absorb any more. Any minute, she was going to turn into steam and vanish. But as he lifted her and took his mouth on a journey down to her stomach, she discovered she could. Her vision hazed. The world around her became dark. And oh, she could feel him. There was nothing but his mouth, his lips and the vivid sensations he was bringing her.

The water was cool on his skin, but she was so hot that his legs had begun to weaken again. His arms, too, he thought as he lowered her into the water. Time was running out. He shifted her, wrapping her legs around him once more.

"Jordan."

Her eyes opened and locked on his. They were still clouded with the pleasure he'd brought her.

"I'm going to take you now."

Her voice was thick when she spoke. "Let's take each other."

That simple sentence very nearly had his knees buckling. Gripping her hips, he slipped inside her. His heart nearly stopped when he felt her heat slip over him, sur-round him.

For a moment as her legs locked tightly around him, he swayed, stunned by the need that shot through him. If it hadn't been for the water, he would have raced hard to the finish. But he couldn't. Neither could she, though he could see she was trying.

Hampered by the water, the rhythm they created was slow, steady. As he looked into her eyes, he knew she was his. He was hers. And all the time, the pleasure built and built. When it was about to peak, he gripped her close against him and staggered with her to the edge of the pool. Kneeling, he settled her beneath him in the shallows and took her mouth with his.

Finally, they could both move the way they wanted to, had to. Faster and faster. His mouth was still pressed to hers when she tightened impossibly around him and cried out his name. His, he thought. He joined her in a shattering release.

AN HOUR LATER, Cash rode side by side with Jordan through the winding canyon. It was closing in on seven o'clock and he figured they had a couple of hours of daylight left. Still time enough to see if they could locate Pete. They'd lingered near the pond longer than they should have, but he'd been reluctant to leave. She'd been so carefree while they'd been there.

After they'd shared the sandwiches he'd packed, they'd taken a swim and then made love once more. But when they'd mounted up, Jordan had grown silent again. She was regrouping. And unless he was mistaken, she was building up a little wall of protection around herself.

From what little she'd said about her mother, he was coming to understand that Eva Ware had been totally focused on her work. He'd seen the same characteristic in

Maddie. But Maddie had grown up with a father who'd spent a lot of time with her. A father who'd enjoyed spending time with his daughter.

He was guessing that Jordan hadn't grown up with a parent like that. It had made her cautious. He figured with a little time, he could work his way around cautious. Problem was, all he had was a little time.

"Penny for your thoughts," he said.

She glanced at him. "We'll have to turn back soon, won't we?"

That hadn't been what she was thinking, but he let it pass. "I figure we can go another mile or so. If we don't locate Pete tonight, I'll send one of my men out tomorrow to make a thorough sweep of the canyon."

She nodded and turned her head to search the canyon walls. "There seem to be more caves in this section."

"Some of them are rumored to be old turquoise mines. That's why Pete frequents the place. Navajos were mining turquoise in New Mexico long before the Spaniards and the white man settled here."

When they turned the next corner of the canyon, they saw a horse, standing to one side.

Cash urged his own mount forward. "That's Pete's horse."

As they approached, the horse whinnied and pawed the ground. Cash scanned the cliffs. Without any direct sunlight, the walls on either side were deeply shadowed. It was Jordan who finally spotted something.

"Up there." She pointed a finger. "I see something red."

"Pete always wears a red neckerchief. It's his trademark." Cash dismounted and anchored his reins with a few rocks. "Stay with the horses. I'll climb up and see."

It took him only a few minutes to reach the ledge of rock where Pete lay. The old man was white as a sheet. His breathing was thready and ragged, but there was a steady pulse at his throat. Cash glanced behind him and called down to Jordan, "He's alive."

Then he glanced above. There was a ledge about fifty feet above him. From the looks of it, the old man had taken a fall.

He considered his options. He didn't know how badly Pete was hurt, and the cliff he'd just climbed up was tricky enough without carrying someone down on his shoulder.

He took out his cell. They were nearly at the point where the canyon passed onto Landry land. The satellite signal should be stronger here than it had been on the Farrell Ranch. He said a brief prayer and punched in a number.

It rang twice. On the third ring, Shay Alvarez picked up. Cash explained the situation. "I'm about a half mile from where the canyon empties onto Landry land. We don't have much daylight left."

"I'll have someone there as soon as I can. If you can build some kind of signal fire, it will help."

Turning, he yelled to Jordan. "Help is on the way."

"There's a blanket on the back of his horse," she called. "I'll bring it up."

It was while he was waiting for Jordan to join him that he noticed how battered and bloody Pete's hands were— as if someone had stomped on them. He glanced up at the face of the cliff above him. Not a fall, he thought.

When Jordan reached him, he showed her the damage to the old man's hands.

"It wasn't an accident," she said.

"Doesn't look like it." He tucked the blanket around Pete, then said, "Why don't you stay with him while I build a signal fire."

Saying nothing, she knelt and gently covered one of the man's battered hands with hers.

No panic. No questions. She was some woman, Cash thought as he climbed back down to the horses.

10

TWO HOURS LATER, Jordan paced in a waiting room. The medics had been fast and efficient, arriving on the scene in just over thirty minutes. Then she and Cash had had to ride the horses back to the ranch and drive into Santa Fe.

They were on the outskirts when her cell phone had rung. She'd thought it might be Maddie and wondered just how much she should tell her sister, but it had been Jase's brother D.C. His plane had landed. She'd filled him in on where they were headed and why, and he'd agreed to meet them at the hospital.

She wasn't alone in the room. Nearby, a woman sat patiently knitting, and there were groups scattered throughout the area, some engaged in hushed conversation, others silently drinking coffee. Occasionally a man or a woman in scrubs would enter the room and approach one of the groups.

In a corner, a TV offering a continuous and muted loop of news hung from a bracket. She glanced out the open archway to a nurse's station where she could see Cash attempting to charm information out of one of the aides.

Usually, pacing helped get her thoughts in order. But she was having trouble getting her mind around the series of events that had occurred since she'd first walked through the front door of her father's ranch.

Was the attack on Pete Blackthorn related to the vandalism that had been happening at the ranch? To the attacks on her? Or was it merely a coincidence that someone had shoved him off that cliff and then made sure that he couldn't climb up or down again?

She'd had time to study his hands before the helicopter had arrived to transport him. They were badly bruised, bloodied and swollen. One of them might have become that seriously injured in a fall, but not both.

Over and over again in her mind, she'd tried to figure out what might have happened. The ledge they'd found Pete on was about halfway up the cliffside. There was what looked to be a cave opening near the top. If he'd simply lost his balance, there were several ledges where he might have landed and gotten a handhold. Someone had made sure he'd fallen a second time.

He'd regained consciousness just as the medics were loading him into a stretcher. For just a second, she'd seen a light of recognition come into his eyes. And then he'd said her sister's name, the sound thready and faint. "Maddie?"

Moving to one of the windows, she stared out at the night. He was going to be all right. He had to be all right.

She nearly jumped when Cash put a hand on her shoulder. When she turned to face him, she saw that Shay Alvarez had joined him.

"Any news?" Jordan asked.

"They've stabilized Pete," Cash said. "But according to the nurse, he's still in line waiting for an MRI. The hospital's a bit backed up because of a tractor-trailer accident, and there are a couple of people with more serious injuries ahead of him. Shay here is the one with news."

"My men found evidence at the scene that backs up your theory that Pete's fall wasn't an accident," Shay said. "There are a string of caves that run along that section of the canyon wall, and in one of them, they discovered cigarette butts. Since Pete doesn't smoke, we think someone else was up there, perhaps waiting for him."

Jordan glanced at Cash, then back at Alvarez. "Why?"

"That's the question," Shay said. "Lea Dashee and her mother are Pete's next of kin. When I contacted Lea to tell her about Pete's fall, she told me that he'd mentioned something to her about six months ago. He'd said he had a feeling that someone was following him. No proof. No solid evidence. A few minutes ago, she called me back. She'd stopped by his trailer on her way here to pick up some things for him. The place had been trashed."

"Six months ago is just about the time that the vandalism started on Maddie's ranch," Cash said.

Shay nodded.

"There's a connection," Jordan insisted.

"Maybe. Maybe not," Shay said.

"Why? Why would someone do that to Pete?" Jordan pressed her fingers to her temples. She was beginning to feel like a parrot that only knew one word.

"Not for the turquoise he's been collecting," Shay said. "He had several packets of them in his saddlebags. Whoever helped him off that cliff didn't rob him. The only other possibility that occurs to me is the belief around here that he has old maps of the turquoise mines that his ancestors once worked. Someone may have gotten the idea they were valuable. That may have been why he was being followed. If indeed he was."

"Is there any way to figure out if the thief found any old maps?" Jordan asked.

Shay smiled. "If I know Pete, they didn't find any. I doubt he'd keep anything that valuable in his trailer, not when he spent so much time away from it, or in his saddlebags. And if he felt he was being followed, he was forewarned."

Over Shay's shoulder, Jordan saw a tall man using a cane step through the waiting room door. "D.C.," she said as she hurried forward, her arms outstretched.

"YOUR COMPETITION?" Shay asked.

Cash studied the tall man in the doorway. "D. C. Campbell, her roommate Jase's brother."

There was nothing in the friendly hug Jordan and D.C. exchanged that even hinted at a more passionate or intimate relationship. So why the hell did he have this coppery, bitter taste in his mouth? "He's on leave from Iraq where he's been serving as an MP, and he's flown out here at his brother's request to provide backup."

"Good idea."

Cash continued to watch as Jordan tucked her arm into D.C.'s and led him over. The cane and the slight limp didn't seem to bother D.C. much.

"Your leg," she said. "How bad is it?"

D.C. smiled at her. "Just a little collateral damage. The army sent me home for a few months to get it rebuilt." He tapped his thigh with one hand. "They replaced a lot of parts. I'm hoping some of them turn out to be bionic."

Jordan laughed. "Stop. I just got a mental image of you leaping over a tall building in a single bound."

"That's what I'm hoping," D.C. said.

Old friends, Cash thought, and something inside of him eased.

After Jordan made the introductions and they shook hands, Cash asked, "How are Jase and Maddie?"

D.C.'s eyes immediately sobered. "I checked in with Jase when I landed, and they were tucked up all safe and sound in a hotel. But there's been a development since I left New York. Earlier this evening, there was a second attempt on Maddie's life. Someone tried to run her down just outside her mother's apartment."

"That's where my mother was killed," Jordan said.

"Yes. The car—a cream-colored sedan—fits the description witnesses gave of the car that struck down Eva Ware. But this time they got a partial plate, and a taxi driver is sure it was a Mercedes."

Jordan stared at him. "That description could fit my mother's car."

"Yes. Jase has a friend at the NYPD who's working to track the car down even as we speak."

"But—" Jordan broke off when there was movement in the doorway and Lea Dashee and an older woman stepped into the room, and Jordan and Shay moved toward them.

"Pete Blackthorn's next of kin," Cash explained to D.C.

"He's the reason Jordan told me to meet you here, right? He's the old man who took a bad fall off a cliff."

"We're sure he was pushed."

"Ah." D.C. pulled a notebook and pen out of his pocket. Then he shot Cash an apologetic glance. "Sorry, old habit."

"No problem. Did Jordan fill you in on the fact that she's masquerading as Maddie while she's here?"

"No." He glanced at Cash. "That could put her in even more danger."

"She felt it was the best way to help her sister out at the big jewelry show tomorrow."

"It may also be helpful in our getting a handle on who's behind all this."

"You think the attacks on Maddie and Jordan are connected."

"Hard not to, but we'll see."

While Cash watched Jordan settle the two women on a couch, he filled D.C. in on what they knew about Pete

Blackthorn and his fall. After pouring coffee and serving the three women, Shay rejoined them.

"Let me see if I got everything," D.C. said. "Pete's been successfully prospecting the land around here as long as anyone can remember, and he reputedly has old maps of the mines his ancestors worked. Starting six months ago, he gets a 'sense' now and then that he's being followed. And today, you suspect someone was waiting for him in one of the caves and pushed him off the cliff."

"That's a good summary," Cash said.

Beyond D.C.'s shoulder, Cash watched Jordan take Lea's hands in hers. He wasn't at all sure how she was managing to hold up through everything. In one day, she'd learned her mother had been murdered, and then her sister's and her own life had each been threatened twice. And right now, her entire focus was on offering some comfort to Maddie's friend, Lea. He was beginning to understand that she'd had a lot of practice coping and taking care of others. Had anyone ever taken care of her?

He turned back to D.C. "Something else you need to know. It was six months ago that the incidents of vandalism began on Maddie's ranch. And six months since Daniel Pearson, our local wannabe real estate mogul, approached Maddie to list the ranch with him. Since then, the seriousness of the vandalism on the ranch has escalated. And this morning someone—we think a pro—tried to run Jordan and me off the road and over a drop-off. Later, there was an incident at the hotel's exhibition hall. The wall of a booth nearly fell on Jordan."

D.C. gave a low whistle as he met the eyes of Alvarez and then Cash. "You didn't mention either of those incidents to Jase."

"No," Cash said as Jordan rejoined them. "We figured he and Maddie had enough on their plates."

For a moment, D.C. glanced down at his notes. "Let's see if I can connect all of the dots here. We've got a man who's made a successful living collecting stones—mostly turquoise—from various abandoned and supposedly tapped-out mines in the area. Someone may have been keeping an eye on him for the last six months, and today this person may have helped him off a cliff. In the same time frame, Maddie is being urged to sell her ranch and there are some incidents perhaps designed to pressure her into doing just that."

"You've got the picture," Cash said.

D.C. scratched his head. "I may be taking a leap here, but what if Pete has at some point discovered a new vein or batch or whatever it's called of turquoise? One that hasn't been tapped out, and what if it's on Farrell land?"

"Not such a big leap," Shay said. "I think we can all make it even without a bionic leg."

D.C. shot him a grin. "Agreed."

"We ran into Pearson today," Cash said. "He seems confident that he's going to close the deal with Maddie tomorrow night over dinner. So why the attack on Pete?"

"Because if Pete gets wind of the fact that Maddie is selling the ranch, he might blab about the existence of a find of turquoise," Shay put in.

"And if she knew about the mine, Maddie wouldn't feel so pressured to sell," Jordan said.

"She wouldn't have to sell—especially if the turquoise is of the quality that Pete has been selling her for years," Cash said.

"The problem is if Pete was attacked so that Maddie would remain under pressure to list the ranch and sell it, why try to kill her? That won't get her signature on the dotted line."

"Good point," Shay said.

"And don't forget that someone's trying to kill Maddie in Manhattan," D.C. put in. "It isn't just one twin who's being threatened."

Shay rocked back on his heels. "The attempts to kill Maddie and Jordan could be unrelated to the sale of the ranch. They could very well have been triggered by the will. It's an open invitation to murder."

"Jase would agree with you on that," D.C. said. "There's a real possibility that there are two things going on here. We were having a similar discussion in my brother's office earlier today. On the surface, there seem to be two things going on in New York, too. Jase and his partner are trying to find the connection between Eva's death and a robbery that occurred at her store about a month ago. And then there are the attempts on Maddie's life."

"And Jordan's. What if it's one big picture, and we just haven't found a way to connect your dots yet?" Cash countered.

A man in a white coat with a stethoscope stuffed in his pocket stepped into the room. "Detective Alvarez?"

Shay moved toward him and guided him to where Lea and her mother were sitting. Jordan hurried to take a seat beside Lea and take her hand.

"He's a strong old man," the doctor began. "The MRI is clear. The X-ray showed no broken bones other than the ones in the hands. He has a good-size bump on his head, but there's no sign of a concussion. We've medicated him for pain and we're treating him for shock and exposure."

"He was unconscious when we first found him," Jordan said.

The doctor nodded. "The medics who brought him in said he was halfway down a cliff. Since his hands were pretty useless, there's no telling how long he might have been lying there before you discovered him. With no way down to his horse, no way to get water, it's not surprising that he was drifting in and out of consciousness. He might have died on that cliff."

Lea Dashee wrapped her arm around her mother's shoulders, then turned to Jordan. "You and Cash saved his life."

Although Jordan had suspected that on some level, hearing the doctor confirm it had her throat drying. What if they hadn't just ridden out? Their original plan had been to tour the ranch on the day after the jewelry show. Pete might not have lasted that long.

"He'll be all right?" Lea asked.

"We think so. We've given him pain medication and a sedative. If his vital signs remain strong overnight, an orthopedic surgeon will operate on his hands tomorrow morning."

"Can I talk to him?" Shay asked.

The doctor looked at Shay. "He's going to be out for a while, and he needs his rest for tomorrow."

"How about if I stop by before he goes into surgery? We believe he had some help falling off that cliff."

The doctor considered, then nodded as he rose. "Just as long as you don't upset him."

As Shay walked the doctor out, Jordan put her arms around Lea. "You're staying?"

"My mother and I will both stay."

"What about the jewelry show?" Jordan asked. "Can I help out in any way?"

Lea managed a smile. "Oh, I'll be there. My mother will stay with Pete. You should go back to the ranch now. Get some rest. I know you're going to wow them tomorrow."

Cash took Jordan's free hand and drew her to her feet. Quite suddenly, she was exhausted. They were halfway to the door when Lea said, "Maddie."

It took her a beat, and Lea called out the name a second time before Jordan turned.

"Thank you for saving my grandfather's life," Lea said. Then Jordan let Cash draw her out of the room.

HOURS LATER, Cash stood at the window in Maddie's bedroom and watched Jordan sleep. She was curled on her side, her hand tucked under her chin. Moments before he'd been lying next to her. The urge to touch her and wake her so that they could make love again was so strong that he'd forced himself to slide out of bed.

She was exhausted—emotionally, physically. He suspected that it wasn't normal for her. She hadn't had much sleep since she'd arrived in Santa Fe, and he was partly responsible for that. She'd dropped off on the drive to the ranch and had only roused slightly when he'd carried her into the house.

"What?" she'd asked. Her eyes had been glazed.

"We're home," he'd said. "Go back to sleep."

After laying her on Maddie's bed, he'd returned to the kitchen to talk briefly with D.C. Jase's brother had been making himself a sandwich.

"I'd say make yourself at home, but I see you're already doing that," he'd said.

"I usually do," D.C. had replied around a mouthful of food. "They don't feed you on airplanes anymore. Probably just as well."

"When you're done, turn left in the hall. You can take the room at the end."

"You'll be with Jordan, I take it."

Cash hooked his thumbs in the front pockets of his jeans. "You have any objection to that?"

D.C.'s eyes had been steady on his. "Just don't hurt her."

"I'm going to do my best not to. You can pass on the same warning to your big brother with regard to Maddie."

Two beats had gone by before D.C. had given him a brief nod. "Fair enough." Then he took another bite of sandwich. "Got any beer?"

"There's another refrigerator in the pantry."

"Thanks. You can go along to bed if you want. I may be up for a while unwinding. Plane trips rev me up for some reason."

As D.C. turned and made his way to the pantry, Cash said, "I don't like playing a waiting game. I'd like to figure out a way to take a more proactive role in this."

D.C. had turned and grinned at him. "You're a man after my own heart. You think this Pearson's behind the vandalism?"

"I do. And he might very well have attacked Pete."

"There might be a way to get him to reveal himself…I'll sleep on it."

"Me, too."

Then he'd left D.C. to his foraging.

Jordan stirred and then settled again. Cash hadn't slept on it yet, but he'd given it some thought. All he'd come up with was to get Pearson alone and beat the truth out of him. It was hard to think of anyone or anything but Jordan when she was in the same bed with him.

Even now she pulled at his thoughts. The hand resting on her thigh appeared delicate—even more so than Maddie's. But it wasn't. He'd seen the way she'd handled Brutus and felt the strength of those slender fingers on his skin.

He let his gaze drift to her face—that so familiar face. It too looked delicate, fragile, sensitive. It was all of those. *She* was all of those. But beneath all that, she had a strength of purpose and a generous heart. He'd watched her with Pete and with his family. If Lea and her mother hadn't said they were going to stay the night with the old man, Jordan would have insisted on keeping him company.

He'd nearly lost her. The thought frightened him, infuriated him. The impulse filled him again—to take her away somewhere safe. To lift her onto his horse and ride off into the sunset with her, just as if they were characters in one of those Western movies she was so fond of.

But they weren't. And they couldn't run away from reality—not while she was being stalked by a killer.

Without looking, he could tell the sky was beginning to lighten behind him. And he sensed deep in his gut that time was going to run out on them. He thought of Maddie in New York. The attacks on both the twins had escalated. He didn't have to be a security expert or a police detective or even an army MP to know that their would-be killer was getting desperate. And while desperate people could make mistakes, they also could get lucky.

Jordan stirred again, and this time her eyes opened. He watched her run one hand over the space in the bed where he'd been. "Cash?"

"Right here." He moved to the side of the bed.

"I thought you'd gone."

"I'm not going anywhere." He slid in beside her.

Her arms curled around him as she settled her body against his. "Is it time to get up?"

"Not yet." He pulled her closer. "Go back to sleep."

"Aren't you going to seduce me?"

"You need the sleep."

She began to nibble on his lips. "What about you?"

Cash knew what he needed, what he wanted. But everything was happening so fast. He needed time to convince her it was what she wanted, too.

"I want you to love me," she murmured against his mouth.

"I do."

Cash's mind began to reel. The words had slipped out of him, and as his heart tumbled into freefall, he realized that they were true. He did love her. When had it happened? How?

Even as he tried to recall, his body was slowly being seduced. Her lips, softened by sleep, were busy on his, teasing, tormenting. There was something familiar about her touch as her fingers grazed over his skin. And something new about her taste. When had it turned so dark, so addictive?

She brushed her mouth over his eyes, his face, his throat. There were so many things he wanted to tell her. So many questions he wanted the answers to. But now wasn't the time. With her name on his lips, he let himself sink into the sensations.

Using her mouth and hands, she began to work her way down his body, nipping one place, caressing another. Ribbons of fire skipped and skimmed along his nerve endings. Her tongue toyed with his nipples, then moved slowly lower, leaving a trail of ice and searing heat in its wake.

Cash tried to reach for her, but his arms were suddenly heavy. When she finally took the hard length of him into her hands, he felt his bones melt. And as her mouth closed around him, pleasure shot to a peak that bordered on agony.

Helpless. He couldn't move, could barely think. No woman had ever made him helpless before. The feeling streamed through his blood, slithered up his spine and steamed his brain. His world had narrowed to Jordan and the slow, steady movement of her mouth on him.

She'd set out to seduce him, to lose herself in him one more time before they had to face the realities of the day. But every time his breath caught or his skin trembled, her own pleasure shot to new heights. Each time he shuddered or moaned her name, her needs grew stronger. Should she have known that in making a man weak she would become as seduced as he was?

When he closed his hands around her shoulders, she still

didn't want to relinquish control. Moving quickly, she straddled him, then raised her hips and lowered herself onto him. They locked fingers and eyes, but for a moment neither of them moved. It was as if by mutual consent, they wanted to stretch out the moment.

When she finally began to move, she did so slowly, fighting against the urge to quicken the pace. Each time she lowered herself, she felt more of him fill her—more and more until she wasn't sure where she left off and he began. More than anything, she wanted to spin out the time for both of them.

When the first rays of sunshine streamed through the window, Cash gripped her hips and with one last hard thrust shattered both of them.

11

"I'M STUFFED," Jordan said, pressing a hand to her stomach when Cash emptied a fresh skillet of scrambled eggs onto the platter in front of her.

"I'll take some of those off your hands." D.C. dumped half of the eggs onto his plate, then offered the rest to Cash.

Jordan shifted her gaze to Cash as the platter was emptied. "I'd think that D.C.'s possibly bionic leg might be hollow, but you're eating as much as he is."

"It's the cowboy life," Cash said. "We load up when we can. Besides, there's no telling when we'll get a chance to eat anything again today."

Jordan tapped the open catalog in front of her. "The hotel is offering a free buffet lunch to exhibitors and attendees."

"According to your sister, jewelry shows aren't exactly known for their hearty buffet lunches," Cash said.

Because she knew from experience he was right, Jordan made no further comment as the two men made their way through a huge amount of food. She might have eaten more than the one slice of bacon and half a piece of toast if the nerves in her stomach hadn't objected.

"You're going to do a fine job of representing Maddie," Cash said before taking a last swallow of his coffee. "You've been practicing how you're going to display her designs for over an hour. I can tell you she never spent that much time figuring out a display in her life."

The phone rang and Jordan jumped. "Who would be calling now?" It was only shortly after seven. "Maddie?"

Cash slid off his stool and went to the phone. "Yes?"

In the silence that followed he mouthed the word *Shay,* and Jordan's stomach settled a bit. Of course it would be Shay. He had planned to speak to Pete Blackthorn before he went into surgery. She had to get a grip.

"And you're not going to arrest him?"

There was another stretch of silence, and as it lengthened, Cash's frown deepened.

"How's Pete?" she asked as soon as Cash had hung up.

"He's lucid and strong enough that his surgery's been scheduled for nine a.m. Shay got ten minutes with him before they wheeled him off for tests."

"Who isn't Detective Alvarez going to arrest yet?" D.C. asked.

Cash poured more coffee into all the mugs. "Pete didn't recognize the man who pushed him. His attacker shoved him from behind. Luckily, the first fall was short, and Pete grabbed a handhold on a ledge. The man followed, and that's when Pete got a look at him. The description he gave Shay could be Daniel Pearson. According to Shay, it could be someone else. But the diamond on the pusher's pinky finger narrows it some."

"Pearson was wearing a diamond on that finger yesterday," Jordan said.

"Yeah. He asked Pete why someone might have attacked him, but Pete was evasive. Shay thinks Jordan would have a better chance getting him to open up. And by the time Pete gets out of surgery and recovery, Shay hopes to have a DNA report from the lab on those cigarette butts."

"He left cigarette butts behind and let himself be seen by the vic?" D.C. shook his head sadly.

"Shay doesn't want to arrest Pearson or even alert him until he has all his evidentiary ducks in a row."

"I can't fault him there," D.C. said with a shrug. "You do want him to pay."

"I'd like to get my hands on him," Cash said.

There was an angry edge in his tone that had Jordan staring at him. It wasn't often that Cash let his laid-back facade crack.

"Do you think this Pearson will be at the jewelry show?" D.C. asked.

"He said he would stop by," Jordan said. "Margo may drag him along with her."

D.C. smiled at Cash. "That will give us some time to get a little proactive and see what else we can learn before Alvarez arrests him."

Cash's eyes narrowed. "You have a plan?"

D.C. spread his hands palms down on the table. "I have an idea. My leg kept waking me up, so while I waited to fall back asleep, I started thinking. One of the things we want to know is if Daniel Pearson has a specific client who wants to buy Maddie's ranch. I'm betting he does."

Cash nodded his agreement.

"A client who had knowledge of the turquoise mine we speculate might exist," D.C. continued. "Otherwise, why would Pearson develop and execute this elaborate plan of escalating vandalism to pressure Maddie into listing the ranch? Especially a ranch that was already struggling to keep afloat."

"That makes sense," Jordan said. "And as far as we know, Pete is the only person who might be able to confirm the existence of such an untapped mine."

"Exactly. While we're waiting for that, my plan is to put some pressure on Pearson. I'm wondering what he would do if he learned he had some competition—someone else who wanted to buy the ranch."

"Who?" Jordan asked.

"None other than one of my buddies during my last tour in Iraq. Greg Majors. His father is rolling in oil money. He's back home now and is always looking for some kind of investment or other."

Cash's eyes narrowed. "And Greg is going to go along with this?"

"Nah," D.C. said. "We're just going to pretend he is. I'll impersonate him, walk up to Jordan's booth, turn on my Texas charm and give her an outrageous offer for the ranch. We just want to spook Pearson. I'm betting if he's threatened or if he thinks there might be a bidding war on the ranch, he'll call his client ASAP. Then we steal his cell and get the number."

There was silence in the room for several seconds.

"It sounds crazy, but it might work," Cash said. "Who's going to lift the cell?"

D.C. grinned. "I think I can handle it. The cane gives me the perfect excuse to stumble up against him."

Jordan looked from one man to the other. "You two are serious."

D.C. turned to her. "It will give us something to do besides sit on our hands while we wait for Shay to get his evidence in order."

"I have plenty to do representing Maddie's jewelry," Jordan said.

"And you can still do it," Cash said. "It shouldn't interfere with the show at all. We'll work around you."

She wasn't going to talk them out of it. She could see it in their eyes. They reminded her of two boys planning some mischief on the playground. Except this was for real. And there was a killer out there.

Cash reached over and took her hand. "We're going to need to know who Pearson's client is. He or she may be the missing dots that we need to complete picture. And until we get that picture, yours and Maddie's lives are still in danger."

"Okay," Jordan said. "But I have a suggestion, something I'd like to modify about your scenario."

"What?" D.C. asked.

Leaning forward, she told them.

CASH STOOD at the back of Jordan's booth. From where he'd positioned himself, he could see anyone who approached her. He also had a good view of the entrance to the hotel's exhibition hall. The transformation that had taken place in the past twenty hours or so was nothing short of a miracle.

The chaos of yesterday had vanished. In its place were neat rows of booths, two running the length of the room, the others stationed at intervals along three sides. Jordan's occupied a central position along the back wall.

In a corner close to the entrance, overstuffed sofas and chairs were clustered and flanked by carved wooden tables. Diagonally across the huge hall from the seating area were tables covered in white linen and laden with trays of chilled fruit, water bottles and coffee. The necks of champagne bottles peeped invitingly out of huge silver buckets. In another corner of the room, a string quartet played something classical and muted.

Jordan stood a few feet away from him, totally focused on adding the final touches to her display. She'd gotten her request for two glass cases, and it had taken her a good ten minutes to arrange the silk scarves she'd brought. Now she was fiddling with the jewelry. She was being as meticulous with the display as her sister had been in designing the pieces.

Cash was willing to bet that even her outfit had been

chosen with the idea of marketing Maddie's pieces. The colors were muted, khaki and white, making the green turquoise dangling from her ears and around her throat stand out even more.

A man in a discreet suit walked by. His eyes never strayed to Jordan's display cases; they were scanning the room. Hotel security, Cash decided.

At the moment, D.C. had tucked himself behind the back wall and was doing some research on his laptop. He'd insisted on driving behind them into Santa Fe in his rental car. That way he could provide some extra protection in case anyone tried something along the road. From what Cash could tell, the man never seemed to take a break. He'd asked to be informed the instant Daniel Pearson appeared. Then he would slip out a back way and return through the main entrance as Greg Majors.

For his part, Cash was content to lean against the wall and just keep watch. It was five minutes until the show opened to the public. Exhibitors with catalogs in hand strolled by, greeted old friends and browsed the displays of newcomers.

Lea had come by earlier to report that her grandfather had been lucid and in good spirits when they'd wheeled him off to the OR. That Pete Blackthorn was alive was a miracle.

When Jordan straightened and backed away a step from the case, he moved to her. "Three minutes until show time."

"I'm ready."

He ran a finger down the bright slivers of turquoise dangling from her ear. "I never doubted it."

She glanced back at the glass cases. "Her designs are so lovely."

Cash studied the display. In each case, she'd clustered pieces in three areas. In one, a circle of earrings and a trio of bracelets were arranged at each end. In the other, a group of pins sat at one end while tie clips and hammered silver belt buckles filled the other. Center stage in each glass case was a necklace.

On his left sat a simple chain of hammered silver rings. The pendant hanging from it was a star studded with turquoise ranging in shades from green to bright blue. The other necklace was made of turquoise beads in varying shades, with an intricately designed silver pendant that made him think of a breastplate a female warrior might wear into battle. Feminine. Strong.

"She's so talented." Jordan's voice was laced with pride as she tapped her finger on the top of the case holding the warrior piece. "This one's my favorite."

"I like it, too."

When she turned back to him, he gave her earring a flick. "You're not a bit jealous of her, are you?"

She stared at him. "Why would I be?"

"Because she obviously inherited your mother's gift for design."

A frown formed on her forehead. "I'm happy for her. I just regret that she and my mother will never get a chance to meet. It's such a waste. All the while I was working on this display, I kept thinking my mother had a fifty-fifty chance of choosing Maddie when they split us up. But it didn't work out that way. I feel so bad for Maddie. For my mother, too."

It was his turn to frown. "What about you, Jordan? Don't you wish you'd grown up here in Santa Fe with your father?"

She thought for a minute. Cash could almost hear the wheels turning. Then she shook her head. "No. I wouldn't be who I am today if I hadn't grown up with my mother. I regret that I never knew Mike Farrell, but now that I know the ranch exists, I'll visit often."

Fear rushed through Cash in such a torrent that he very

nearly grabbed her. She spoke so calmly of returning to her life in New York. Couldn't she see that she belonged here in Santa Fe just as much as Maddie did? But at that moment, the doors opened and the first wave of customers poured through. Turning, he let her words echo in his mind.

I'll visit it often.

Could he be happy with that?

STRING MUSIC and ripples of conversation filled the exhibition hall as dealers wove their way from booth to booth. It was two hours into the show and Jordan was almost ready to relax. She'd collected several business cards, answered the same questions over and over and taken dozens of orders. Once she'd noted that the potential clients were especially interested in the jewelry pieces she wore, she'd started rotating other bracelets and earrings from the display cases. But she hadn't disturbed the necklaces. They were generating interest right where they were.

No one as yet had suspected she wasn't Maddie. More importantly, they loved her sister's designs. True, her smile was beginning to ache at the corners of her mouth, but thanks to Maddie's sensible taste in shoes, her feet were still fine.

Then she spotted a man coming toward her with a beaming smile on his face. Obviously, he knew Maddie but she was coming up blank. She shot a glance back at Cash. He'd helped her out before, but as the visitor moved toward her, Cash said softly, "Don't have a clue."

The man was small and round, with rimless glasses perched on his nose. He had kind eyes, and she saw in them the light of an old friendship. Who was he?

"Ms. Farrell." He extended his hand and she shook it.

"Maddie," she said automatically. "I'm so glad you came."

"Ah, there they are." Perhaps it was the slight Hispanic accent or maybe it was the way he leaned over to study the necklace centered in the first case, but the memory slipped into place. This had to be Joe Manuelo, the man who cut and polished Maddie's stones. Maddie had explained in her notes that when she got stones from a mine, she always took them to Manuelo, whose family had been in the business for years, and he often visited her shows.

"Beautiful," he murmured as he glanced up at her again. "Could I hold it?"

"Of course, Mr. Manuelo."

"Joe."

She beamed a smile at him as she opened the case and lifted it out. He took it carefully, then holding it in one hand, he removed his glasses and studied it more closely. "Are you happy with the way I cut the stones?"

"Thrilled. You did a marvelous job."

"Thank you." He handed her back the necklace. "I like to see what happens to the stones after they leave my shop. I admire the way you've mixed the various shades. But you have old Pete to thank for the quality of the stones. What you've been sending me lately—the hardness, the quality—are exceptional. It makes my work easy."

Of course, he would know Pete Blackthorn was her source, Jordan thought. "Pete's been hurt."

Joe Manuelo immediately frowned. "Hurt? How badly?"

Jordan told him what she knew.

"Someone pushed him off a cliff?" There was a mix of shock and anger on his face.

"That's what we think. The police are looking into it."

"They'd better find out who did it."

"Lea Dashee might know the latest on his condition."

"Thank you, Ms. Farrell. I had it in mind to look at some

of her designs. too." With a final nod, he hurried off in the direction of Lea's booth.

She felt Cash's hands on her shoulders. "Pete has a lot of friends," he said.

"And at least one enemy," she added.

An hour later, the crowds had thinned. Cash assumed the dealers would be taking advantage of the buffet lunch the hotel was providing for them. Then, according to Jordan, they'd be back for a final push. He studied her as she switched the necklace and earrings she was wearing for a new set from the cases.

Whatever nerves she might have had at the beginning of the show had faded. When she talked about Maddie's designs, there was an energy that emanated from her. She might not be a designer, but she knew how to talk the talk. And there wasn't a doubt in his mind that she was enjoying herself. No one watching her would ever suspect that her life and her sister's had been threatened more than once in the past twenty-four hours. By any standards, she was a remarkable woman.

He'd moved forward to tell her just that when he saw Daniel Pearson and Margo Lawson entering the exhibition hall. Margo had her nose in the catalog, and by the time she pointed in their direction, Daniel had already spotted them.

Cash backed up, slipped one hand behind him, and tapped lightly on the wall of the booth. "Showtime, D.C." Then he leaned back and prepared to enjoy himself.

Three hours of handling dealers and gawkers had brought color to Jordan's cheeks. She looked perfectly at ease as Margo and Pearson reached her booth. Margo sent him a look, but then she leaned over the case to study the collection. Clearly, she was focused on business before pleasure.

Pearson barely glanced at the display cases before he took one of Jordan's hands. The diamond on his pinky finger caught the light. "Lovely job. Our dinner reservations are for six-thirty here in the hotel. I thought after the show, you'd enjoy someplace close."

And the sooner he could get her signature on the dotted line, the better, Cash thought. He'd been working Maddie for months. Why the sudden rush? Perhaps the answer to that question lay in the little charade they were about to enact.

When he realized his hands had fisted, Cash relaxed them. Out of the corner of his eye, he saw D.C. making his way toward them. The only thing that Cash didn't like about the little scenario Jordan and D.C. had finally decided on was that his job wasn't a more active one. He was supposed to observe Pearson's reactions.

"I have to have this one." Margo pointed at the center piece in the second case. "You've never designed anything quite like it before."

"No sense in bringing the same old, same old to a show," Jordan said.

"You haven't sold it. Tell me you haven't."

Jordan beamed Margo a smile. "I've sold three of them, as a matter of fact."

Margo's face registered disappointment. "But then they won't be unique. My customers don't want to see themselves coming and going."

"But each one *will* be unique. The colors of the turquoise stones will vary. Look at the color variations in this other necklace." She gestured to the other case. "So will the color of the beads in the necklace. And the shape of the pendant will vary also. I've made some sketches. See."

Margo studied the sketches Jordan placed on the case. Then she turned her attention back to the necklace. Finally, she met Jordan's eyes. "Yes, I can see. Brilliant. When did you come up with that marketing strategy?"

Jordan shrugged. "When three different dealers asked for a unique necklace."

"Make that four."

Cash bet it was Jordan who'd come up with the strategy and not Maddie.

Pearson had begun to fan himself with his catalog. Bored to tears, Cash thought.

D.C. was closing in. Cash bet that Pearson wouldn't be fanning himself much longer.

"Ms. Farrell?"

The drawl was unmistakably Texas. The charm, Cash was beginning to suspect, was D. C. Campbell.

Jordan shook D.C.'s extended hand.

"I'm Greg Majors." D.C.'s grin was apologetic. "Of course, you don't know me from Adam, but I have a business card." He fished it out of a pocket and passed it to her. "I'm here representing Majors Limited. My daddy owns a bunch of oil wells in Texas, and he's always looking for ways to invest his excess cash flow."

Jordan looked a little confused. "Does he want to invest in my jewelry business?"

D.C. glanced down at the display cases. "I could certainly suggest that to him." Then he met Jordan's eyes. "But I'm here to talk to you about your ranch."

Every bone in Pearson's body stiffened. Good, Cash thought.

"Now wait just a minute," Pearson said.

D.C.'s good ol' boy charm didn't falter for a second. "And you are?"

"Daniel Pearson of Montgomery Real Estate."

D.C. nodded. "Good to meet you. Are you representing Ms. Farrell's interests here?"

"Yes."

D.C. pulled out his notebook, flipped it open. "I'm sorry. Has she listed her ranch with you? I don't see that in my notes."

"No. She hasn't. But—"

D.C. cut him off with a raised palm and turned back to Jordan. "Ms. Farrell, my daddy is interested in investing in a string of select properties and turning them into an elite group of vacation destinations. In your case, we're thinking of a dude ranch. It wouldn't interfere with the running of the ranch, nor would it change the landscape in any significant way. My daddy started out as a rancher, and that's where his heart still is. But if it hadn't been for the black gold that he discovered on his land…well, the Majors family wouldn't be where it is today. We've done our research on you."

And Pearson was doing research, too. His fingers were busy on the BlackBerry he'd pulled out of his pocket. Taking two easy steps forward, Cash was able to see that he'd pulled up the Majors Limited Web site. If Pearson decided to dig deeper, D.C.'s cover story would check out. He'd seen to it by contacting his old buddy on their way into town.

"You want to buy my ranch?" Jordan asked, doing her best to look confused.

"No, not at all. We want to invest in your ranch and in you."

As D.C. elaborated on his plan, Cash began to relax. Her modification of D.C.'s initial plan was working. Not only was it driving Pearson into panic mode, but what D.C. was describing to her were all her ideas. Cash was beginning to think that she was serious about turning the Farrell Ranch into a working dude ranch. One thing he was certain of. She and D.C. should be nominated for some award. The Daytime Emmys?

"We'll provide advice, financial support, advertising and

marketing help," D.C. was explaining. "We think that offering vacations on a working ranch will have great appeal."

Jordan pressed hands to her temples. "Wait. I get to keep the ranch, run cattle, do everything I'm doing now?"

D.C. beamed a smile at her. "That's the plan. And it will be just the attraction that draws your guests. Lots of dude ranches around. Very few offer a true ranch experience. Add quality accommodations and gourmet food…" He raised both hands and dropped them. "Daddy and I think it's a win-win idea. Good for a small rancher trying to make ends meet. Good for us."

"Maddie, we need to talk about this. You don't know this man." Pearson's knuckles had turned white where he was gripping his BlackBerry, and there was a thread of panic in his voice.

Jordan gave him a distracted glance. "Of course. But not now." Then she refocused her attention on D.C.

"My daddy and I have already opened a few. Our plan is to have a chain of them operating across the Southwest—Nevada, New Mexico, Colorado. But this isn't the place to go into details. How about we meet after the show is over—say around six or six-thirty? I have a suite on the top floor. We can grab a bite to eat."

Pearson nearly choked. "Maddie, *we* have dinner plans at six-thirty."

Jordan's eyes, her voice, were apologetic. "Daniel, I have to hear more about this. You know I don't want to have to sell the ranch. I have to see if this could be a possibility for me."

"Fine. But you're making a mistake." Pearson stalked away, and with an apologetic smile, Margo hurried after him. He was punching in numbers on his BlackBerry even as he detoured to the cluster of sofas at the far corner of the room.

Cash put some effort into staying right where he was. It would have been too bad to destroy their little charade now. But he'd been the only one looking at Pearson when Jordan had put their dinner meeting on hold. For one instant, the real estate broker's smooth facade had cracked. Cash had caught a glimpse of the fury and panic, and it hit home that they might have put Jordan in even more danger.

"I'll see you around six," D.C. said, staying in his role. Cash noted that there were a few dealers around who'd become interested once Pearson had raised his voice.

"I'll give you my suite number." After scribbling something on a card, he handed it to her.

When Cash stepped forward, he read the two words D.C. had written. *Be careful.* He met the other man's eyes for a moment and nodded. They were on the same page where Pearson was concerned. That was the problem with stirring up a hornet's nest, Cash thought. There was always a chance that you'd get more trouble than you wanted.

With a final nod, D.C. moved slowly toward the door as if slowed down by his cane. He timed it perfectly, reaching the exit and turning back just as Pearson bolted toward it. The collision looked perfect. A man with a cane was knocked on his backside. Pearson made a hurried apology and with Margo following, he left the exhibition hall.

Since several people, a few of them security, had clustered around D.C., Cash stayed where he was. A moment later, D.C. had settled himself on one of the sofas and appeared to be making a call on his cell.

"Hopefully, we'll have a clue." Cash spoke softly to Jordan. "It would be too bad to waste a performance like that."

Her eyes were on the display case, but her lips curved slightly. "I agree. In any case, I think I just canceled my date with Danny Boy Pearson."

"And he's furious," Cash commented. "What I saw in his

eyes was bordering on the irrational." He took her hand in his and squeezed. "He may try to take his temper out on you."

"Then we'll have to be very careful."

CASH SPENT the next half hour switching his attention between Jordan, whose business had once more picked up, and D.C., who spent the time alternating between his laptop and his cell phone.

At one point, shortly after he'd had his collision with Daniel Pearson, D.C. had signaled one of the guards and gestured to a space under one of the couches. The guard dutifully retrieved a BlackBerry and carried it out of the exhibition room. When Pearson missed it, Cash was betting he'd locate it in the hotel's Lost and Found.

Jordan was writing up yet another order when D.C. tucked his laptop under his arm, rose from the couch, and made his way back to the booth.

When he reached them, D.C. spoke in his Greg Majors voice. "Ms. Farrell, I know I said I'd wait until later, but I've got some preliminary figures for you."

Opening his laptop, he set it on one of the cases and angled it toward Jordan. Then he spoke in a voice that didn't carry. "Good news and bad news. The number Pearson called belongs to Rainbow Enterprises Limited. I even retrieved the extension number. But when I dialed it, all I got was a series of automated responses and invites to leave a message."

"So we still don't know who Pearson called or who his client might be?" Cash asked.

"Working on it," D.C. said. "I tried Jase and got his voice mail, but I was able to reach his partner, Dino Angelis. According to Dino, Jase and Maddie are currently out of cell-phone reach while they're tracking down a lead they picked up at Eva Ware Designs. Fortunately,

Dino knows just about as much as my brother does about hacking into records." He patted the laptop before tucking it back under his arm. "I'll be working on it, too. It's only a matter of time before we find out who's behind Rainbow Enterprises."

Cash put some effort into controlling his frustration as he watched D.C. walk away. What he couldn't entirely rid himself of was the feeling in his gut that time was running out on them.

12

IT WAS NEARLY SIX when Jordan and Cash stood outside Pete Blackthorn's hospital room. Since the floor didn't allow cell phones, D.C. had stayed outside the main entrance to check in with Jase's partner again. They still hadn't been able to find out who owned Rainbow Enterprises Limited. Jordan figured the position also gave him a chance to see if anyone had followed them from the hotel. They'd used two cars again, and the police cruiser following them had made it a parade.

Lea had stepped out as soon as they'd arrived to announce the good news. "The surgery took a long time, but his hands are going to be fine. You'll be able to see him as soon as Detective Alvarez is through."

Jordan watched through the window of Pete's room as Lea rejoined her grandfather. Shay was in the process of showing Pete some photos, and the old man was studying each one intently.

Now that the jewelry show was over, she should be feeling relieved. During the closing rush, she'd rung up several impressive sales, some with dealers who'd never bought Maddie's designs before. And she'd taken at least a dozen orders for each of the centerpiece necklaces.

She should want to celebrate. But the nerves in her stomach were still jumping. She'd tried to contact Maddie to tell her the good news, but all she'd gotten was voice mail.

Sensing her tension, Cash ran his hands down her arms, then up again to settle on her shoulders.

"You're just as worried as I am," she said.

"I'll relax once Pearson is behind bars. Whatever or whoever is driving him to take your ranch off your hands has pushed him pretty close to the edge."

"If Pete can identify Daniel's picture, will Shay be able to arrest him?"

"Hopefully. But I'm not sure that will get us all the answers we need."

A man in green scrubs stepped into Pete's room, and a moment later Shay joined them in the hall. His timing perfect, D.C. stepped out of the elevator and walked toward them.

"Time to powwow," he said. "I've got some news from the other coast."

"Are Maddie and Jase all right?" Jordan asked.

D.C. sent her a reassuring smile. "I got everything secondhand from his partner since Jase is currently in an emergency room. Nothing serious. And Maddie's fine." He glanced around. "Anyone mind if we continue this conversation in the hospital cafeteria? I'm starved."

No one objected.

FIFTEEN MINUTES LATER, the four of them were seated at an isolated table in the semicrowded cafeteria. A couple of potted trees blocked them from view on one side, and the scents of hot food and old coffee hung in the air.

Cash and Shay had procured loaded trays, offering a cornucopia of selections—everything from pizza to burgers and tacos. Jordan hadn't realized until she caught the scent of it that she, too, was starved. After she'd downed her pizza, she looked at Shay. "Was Pete able to identify Daniel Pearson?"

"He was."

"You're going to arrest him, then?"

"When I do, I want to be able to hold him. The man who tried to run you off the road yesterday still hasn't regained consciousness, but I've been able to trace his prints. Angelo Ricci. He's a professional from the East Coast—New York, New Jersey."

"I can have Campbell and Angelis Security check into it," D.C. offered. "Jase has a good friend in the NYPD, Detective Dave Stanton. Jase will give him your name."

"I'm obliged. In the meantime, I'm checking out Pearson's alibi for yesterday. Pete claims that he was attacked just as soon as he climbed up that cliff—maybe nine a.m. or so."

"We met up with Daniel Pearson and Margo Lawson in Santa Fe around noon. That would give him plenty of time," Jordan said.

"He didn't check in with Montgomery Real Estate until after that," Shay said around a mouthful of burger. "Still, he impresses me as a careful man. He may very well have established an alibi for himself. And he's socially well-connected. Either he or his lawyers are going to claim that Pete's a confused old man. The sun was probably in his eyes. While we're waiting for the DNA on those cigarette butts to come in, it'd be good if we could establish motive."

Setting his coffee down, Cash turned to D.C. "You got anything yet on that cell phone call he made?"

D.C.'s grin was wide as he pulled his notebook out of his pocket. "As a matter of fact, I do. Rainbow Enterprises Limited is one of many, many small companies owned or at least partially owned by Ware Bank."

"Ware Bank is run by my uncle Carleton," Jordan stated.

"Yep. And your Aunt Dorothy currently heads up Rainbow."

"Aunt Dorothy? As far as I know she's never been involved in Ware Bank—other than to host the annual Christmas party at Ware House."

"Pearson called her?" Cash asked.

"Whether or not he talked directly to her is a question. As far as I could tell, there's no human being on the other end of that line. But he definitely called a company she owns and he could have left a message."

"So Daniel Pearson might have a connection to my Aunt Dorothy?" Jordan asked.

D.C. nodded. "Which is very interesting when you consider that your Aunt Dorothy has just been arrested for killing your mother and attempting to kill Jase and Maddie."

Jordan reached for Cash's hand. "Aunt Dorothy killed my mother?"

"So she says," D.C. said. "She confessed to Maddie right after she took my brother out with a fireplace poker."

Jordan's throat constricted and Cash's grip on her hand tightened. "Jase and Maddie—are they—"

"They're fine. Jase is getting patched up in an emergency room. Maddie came out of their confrontation with Dorothy Ware unscathed."

"But why would Aunt Dorothy kill my mother?"

"Details are sketchy at this point. Both she and Adam Ware have been arrested and are still being questioned by the NYPD."

"Adam's been arrested, too? For what?"

"I can only give you a bare bones version. But about a month ago, Adam robbed Eva Ware Designs of one hundred thousand dollars' worth of jewels in order to cover some gambling debts. When your mother figured that out, she told your cousin that he had to leave Eva Ware Designs, and your aunt didn't believe that failure should be in the cards for a Ware."

"But that's insane." Jordan pressed her free hand to her temple as she watched D.C. and Shay exchange a look.

"I've come across worse excuses for murder," Shay murmured.

"What about Uncle Carleton?" Jordan asked.

"Adam and Dorothy both claim that he knew nothing about their activities," D.C. said.

"So Dorothy Ware killed Eva to protect the Ware name," Cash said. "But why in the world has she been in contact with a real estate agent in Santa Fe for the past six months? And what does she have to do with the attacks on Maddie's ranch and Jordan's life?"

"Ah," D.C. said. "That's the million-dollar question, isn't it?"

THROUGH THE WINDOW, Cash watched as Jordan went in to Pete Blackthorn's room. Lea had come while they were still in the cafeteria to tell Jordan that the old man wanted to speak to her alone. As soon as Jordan finished with Pete, he was going to take her back to the ranch.

D.C.'s news had been a lot to absorb. He imagined Maddie must be struggling with it, too. But Dorothy and Adam Ware were strangers to her. To Jordan, they'd been part of a family she'd known all her life. And because of the two of them, her mother was dead.

When they'd left the cafeteria, D.C. and Shay were making plans to return to his office and contact Jase's friend Detective Stanton directly for the latest update on the investigation there. And Shay intended to get an arrest warrant for Daniel Pearson.

Cash tucked his hands in his pockets and tried to relax. They were in the home stretch. As soon as Shay and D.C. nailed down a motive and a definite connection and between Dorothy Ware and Pearson, the threat to Jordan should be over.

Right?

According to D.C., Dorothy Ware had denied orchestrating the attempted hit on Maddie. Instead, she'd tried to run her down with the same car that she'd used to run down Eva Ware—a car that ironically belonged to Jordan's mother.

If Dorothy Ware preferred to handle things by herself, who had hired the man who'd tried to run them off the road yesterday? Or the sniper who'd taken a shot at Maddie?

Something—the same feeling that he often got on cattle drives when he sensed an unseen danger to his herd—told him that it wasn't time to relax his guard yet. Not until they had all the dots connected.

He watched Jordan pull up a chair to Pete Blackthorn's bedside. She was frightened. Cash had felt it in the way she'd gripped his hand on the ride up in the elevator. What that wild ride down the hill yesterday hadn't accomplished, a meeting with an old man had. And it wasn't merely that she was going to ask him about an untapped vein of turquoise. If he was up to answering, she was going to ask him what he knew about her parents' marriage and why they'd separated. And why they'd decided to separate their two daughters.

He wanted those answers, too, he realized. He glanced at the door to Pete's room, which was opened just a crack. He wasn't above eavesdropping to get them. He also wanted to know why Eva had decided to bring her two daughters together only after her own death. He thought he understood why she'd asked them to change places. It was a quick way to force them to get to know one another. And if she had the kind of tunnel vision Jordan had described when it came to her business, she would have wanted Maddie to experience what it would be like to work at Eva Ware Designs.

But had she given even one thought to the fact that she might be putting them in mortal danger with the terms of that will?

He moved closer to the door where he could still keep Jordan in view through the window. He wanted to go to her. He couldn't. All he could do was stand in the background and try to provide what support he could. Her shoulders were just as tense as they'd been when she'd been setting up the display of Maddie's jewelry earlier in the day. But she was just as ready to face what Pete might tell her as she'd been to meet the dealers at the show.

He thought of what she'd been through since she'd changed places with her sister. Jordan Ware was amazing.

PETE'S EYES were closed, so Jordan sat there in silence, not wanting to disturb him. His hands were bandaged and an IV was still attached to one of his arms. He looked even more fragile and vulnerable than he had when she'd sat beside him on that ledge.

Her head was still spinning from the news that D.C. had relayed to them in the cafeteria.

Aunt Dorothy had murdered her mother. And she'd tried twice to kill Maddie. Every time Jordan tried to reconcile those acts with the controlled and sophisticated society matron she'd known all of her life, she began to get a headache. Dorothy Ware was a woman who seemed to have everything she wanted. She was married to a very rich man. She led a prominent social life, one that frequently got her mentioned in the society pages. She served on prestigious cultural and charity boards, and she lived in a mansion.

If it was hard for her to imagine Dorothy as a killer, it was a lot less difficult for her to believe that her cousin, Adam, had developed a gambling problem and decided to turn to a loan shark for help. But that he'd actually had the guts to rob Eva Ware Designs to pay off his debts? That was a shocker.

Secrets, Jordan thought. They seemed to run in her family. Jordan wondered if she'd ever really known any of her relatives—including her mother.

When she saw Pete's eyes flutter open, nerves and excitement began to dance in her stomach. Maybe he would be able to expose some of them.

"Ah, you're here." His voice was surprisingly strong for a man who'd gone through what he had in the past two days. "Wondered if I'd ever get to see you again."

"You're going to be fine," Jordan hastened to say. "The doctors—"

"My granddaughter has filled me in on my prognosis," Pete interrupted. "Even though there's nothing wrong with my hearing. Dr. Salinas explained that with time I should recover eight-five percent use of both hands. I got it."

Jordan bit back a smile at the cranky tone.

"Need to tell you some things," he said. He jerked his head at the IV drip "—and there's no telling when the stuff they're pumping into me will have me falling asleep again."

"I'm listening," Jordan said. "And if you doze off, I'll wait right here until you wake up again."

"Good." Pete narrowed his eyes on her. "First, tell me where Maddie is."

Jordan had to work to keep her mouth from dropping open. What she read in his eyes sent any thought of continuing with her masquerade flying. "She's in Manhattan. How did you know I wasn't Maddie?"

A trace of a smile flickered briefly on his face. "Wish I could tell you I recognized you. But I stopped by the ranch a few days ago, and your sister left notes by the phone. Wanted to tell her something. Your name was there on a pad by the phone along with a reservation number for a flight to New York. When I came to on the cliff and noticed your hair was different, I figured you for Jordan."

Jordan felt her stomach take a little tumble. "You knew about me, then?"

"Held you in my arms when you were a baby. Your sister, too. Your grandfather and I were close friends. He let me prospect anywhere I wanted to on his land. When he passed on, your dad was in his twenties. I took to stopping by to see how he was doing. Not that he needed anyone to keep tabs on him. Mike Farrell was born to be a rancher. And occasionally, he could even beat me at chess."

"So you knew my mother?"

"Yes. Surprised me that she decided to put the two of you in contact after all these years."

Jordan moistened suddenly dry lips. "Why did they separate us? Do you know?"

He frowned then. "Your mother didn't tell you?"

Jordan shook her head. "She can't. She's dead." Then she gave Pete the *Reader's Digest* version of the terms of her mother's will and what had happened so far.

When she finished, he shook his head. "Hard on the two of you. I never did agree with what Mike did. Advised him against it. But he loved her. I'm not suggesting that she didn't love your father. She did. But to my way of thinking, he loved her more. And when he realized he had to let her go, you were the one gift he insisted on giving her."

"What?"

"He gave her you."

"I don't understand."

Pete shook his head sadly. "Neither did I. Eva was just out of college when she came out to Santa Fe. There was a job her family wanted her to take back on Long Island, but she didn't want it. What she wanted was for them to finance her so that she could start her own business as a jewelry designer. But when her brother and her father ganged up against her, she took what money she had and ran away to follow her dream. She came to Santa Fe because she wanted to study the Native American designers and work with turquoise. She and Mike met one day, and it was love at first sight. The kind you read about in books. You understand?"

Jordan nodded. A ripple of fear moved through her because she thought she did.

"Everything was fine—just like the fairy tales. Three weeks to the day after they met, they got married."

"Three weeks?"

"Twenty-one days. Mike crossed them off on a calendar. He'd wanted to tie the knot on day two, but she'd insisted they wait. In three weeks they'd be more certain of what they wanted. After the wedding, Mike built her a studio so that she could design jewelry to her heart's content. Then she got pregnant. Mike was ecstatic. She wasn't. Morning sickness kept her from her work. And when it passed, she buried herself in her studio as if she was racing against the clock."

Knowing her mother, Jordan thought she understood. "Eva was a very focused person. She was probably worried that becoming a mother would interfere with her goal of becoming a top designer."

"That's the way Mike explained it. But she withdrew from him, too."

"And after Maddie and I were born?"

"Whatever worries she had only grew. You were six months old when she told Mike she had to leave. She was going back to New York. He could have custody of the two of you. She wouldn't contest it. She wouldn't even ask for visitation rights."

"She wanted to leave us both here on the ranch?" For a moment, Jordan let herself wonder what that might have been like—to have grown up with a twin and a father and not her mother.

Pete nodded. "But Mike wouldn't agree. That's when he came up with the plan. He would give her the start-up money for her jewelry business, and he would let her go back to New York. But in return, she had to take one of you with her."

"Why?"

"Beats me. He tried to explain. He said he loved her and he wanted her to have someone in her life to care about besides her designs. He wanted her to have someone in her life who would love her."

Jordan swallowed away the lump in her throat. As difficult as it was, she thought she could understand her mother's panic. All her life Eva Ware been driven by a dream—to become a top designer. And for the first time since she'd come to the ranch, Jordan thought she might be coming to know her father. He was a man who was capable of great love—of his land and his heritage, of his daughters and of the woman he'd fallen in love with.

Her father had given her up so that Eva wouldn't be alone.

"I told him he was crazy—especially after she insisted that if she did take one of you, the other could never know about it. There was to be no contact."

"One child was enough," Jordan said, nodding.

"That's the way I saw it. She didn't want to be involved in visits or in dealing with trips when the two of you would want to be together. She wanted a clean break. I told your father he was a fool to agree. But he loved her."

"Very much, it seems." And she thought her mother, whatever she had accomplished in her life, had been a fool to turn away from that kind of love.

Unable to remain seated any longer, Jordan rose and

began to pace back and forth beneath the windows. But she turned when Cash entered the room, and when he crossed to her she simply stepped into his arms.

Safety, she thought as the warmth stole into her. And understanding. If this was what her mother had found with Mike Farrell, how had she ever been able to walk away?

"Your father didn't keep to the letter of the bargain," Pete said after a moment. "He sent letters and gifts and pictures of Maddie."

Jordan turned. "She never gave them to me." Suddenly she frowned. "But there were gifts sometimes, surprise presents."

"The toy ranch you talked about," Cash said.

"Yes. And she never objected when I became interested in riding and I wanted my own horse."

"Guilty conscience?" Drawing her with him, Cash moved toward the bed. "Thank you for telling her."

"'Bout time I told someone. Mike swore me to secrecy a long time ago. Your father, too. Shortly before he died, he gave me a sealed letter addressed to both of you. Made me promise I'd deliver it if you ever found each other. After Mike died, I thought long and hard about giving it to Maddie and telling her she had a sister. But a promise is a promise."

"Did anyone else know about the twins?" Cash asked. "Other than you and my parents?"

Pete frowned thoughtfully. "I don't think so." He shifted his gaze from Jordan to Cash. "Thanks for bringing me in here. I owe you one."

Cash smiled slowly. "I think I'll collect right now. Tell me about the fresh vein of turquoise you've been mining on Maddie's ranch."

Pete winced. "That's something Mike swore me to secrecy on, too. I discovered it years ago, right about the same time he met and married Eva. The deal was that I could work it for as long as I wanted. But I couldn't tell anyone where I was getting the stones."

"He never filed a claim?" Cash asked.

Pete shook his head. "Not Mike Farrell. He didn't want any of the big mining companies out at his ranch sniffing around. He didn't want the land harmed in any way."

"So part of Maddie's heritage is that she owns a turquoise mine?" Jordan asked.

"Yep. And it's a damn rich one, too."

13

IT WAS FULLY DARK when Cash turned his pickup down the road that led to the ranch. D.C. was about five minutes behind them in his rental car. He'd still been on the phone with Detective Stanton when they'd left him in Shay's office.

The NYPD was getting closer to wrapping up their cases against Adam and Dorothy Ware. Though both continued to deny having hired any hit people or having any connection to Rainbow Enterprises Limited, both had connections to John Kessler, Adam's loan shark, who could easily have put either of them in touch with a paid assassin. And to Cash's way of thinking, both Dorothy and Adam certainly had motive to kill Maddie and Jordan. If the twins were both eliminated, according to the terms of Eva's will, Dorothy, Adam and Carleton would each get an even bigger slice of the pie that was Eva Ware's estate.

Maddie and Jase were still out of cell-phone contact at the hospital, but Dino Angelis was using every resource he had at Campbell and Angelis Security to check into both Dorothy's and Adam's e-mail and phone records.

They'd left Shay questioning Daniel Pearson. The real estate man had lawyered up as soon as he'd been brought in. Faced with the DNA results on the cigarette butts, he admitted to having been in the area where Pete had been found, but he vehemently denied that he'd been there that morning. He had confessed that he did indeed have a buyer for the Farrell Ranch, but the only contact he'd had with his client was through a spokesperson for Rainbow Enterprises Limited.

Shay was having two of his men check Pearson's alibi. Since it promised to be a long night, Cash hadn't objected when Jordan had asked if they could return to the ranch.

She'd been dead on her feet. Little wonder. Still, she hadn't fallen asleep on the ride from Santa Fe. He suspected that she was just as wired as he was. He figured he wasn't going to get much shut-eye until he could be sure that the danger for Jordan was over.

And he wasn't sure that it was. He thought of D.C.'s analogy to a connect-the-dots puzzle. To his way of thinking, they still didn't have a clear picture. If it turned out that neither Dorothy Ware nor Adam had hired the hit woman in New York or the man who'd tried to drive them off the road yesterday, who had?

As they rounded a curve in the road, he glanced toward Jordan. "Penny for your thoughts."

"My mind keeps returning to the secrets everyone has been keeping. My aunt, my cousin, my mother. My father, too. All those years of hiding the existence of that turquoise mine. Preserving the integrity of the land and his heritage must have been very important to him."

She paused for a moment as he turned into the drive that led to the ranch house. "You knew him. Would he object to the idea of starting up a dude ranch as a side business? Would that go against what he would have wanted for his land?"

Reaching over, he linked his fingers with hers. "I think he'd go along with it if you believe it's a way that Maddie can make ends meet."

"I don't have it all thought through yet."

"I don't know about that. The way Greg Majors explained it to you at the jewelry show, it sounded pretty good."

She smiled at him. "It did, didn't it? I was really tempted to buy into it. But Maddie won't be able to take it on. I'll have to figure a solution to that."

Cash's heart took a hard thump. "Why not run it yourself, Jordan?"

There was a beat of silence. "I can't be in two places at once. I've thought about the fact that Maddie is now the most obvious choice to step into our mother's shoes as head designer at Eva Ware Designs. But that may not be what she wants. It could be that she'd like to remain independent. In that case, I'll be needed more than ever at my mother's company. We'll have to find a new designer, and I'll have to be there to negotiate the transition."

"And you seem to be equally committed to find a solution so that Maddie can keep the ranch."

"I am."

"Perhaps neither one of you are going to be able to return completely to your own lives. Maybe that's why your mother gave you twenty-one days."

"According to Pete, she needed that amount of time to be sure she was making the right decision in marrying my father. Clearly, it wasn't a magic number."

"Who's to say it wasn't?" Cash countered. "If Mike Farrell and Eva Ware had never married, neither you nor Maddie would be here. However much you may judge them for the decisions they made later, they both took a risk. And you were the result. Who's to say that it was wrong?"

For a couple of beats, Jordan said nothing, and something around Cash's heart tightened. Finally, she said, "We still have about nineteen days left to work out the details."

Cash had always thought he was a patient man, but to his way of thinking, nineteen days might be too long for him to wait. There were details that he wanted to nail down right away.

But it was the wrong time to push her. As he rounded the last curve in the drive, the shadowy outlines of the ranch buildings came into view. "That's odd."

"What?"

"The floodlights aren't on. They usually only go off during a power failure." He braked to a stop in front of the ranch house and they both climbed out.

Cash smelled it first. The faintest sting in the air. He glanced at Jordan and saw that she'd caught it, too.

"Smoke," he said as he scanned the outbuildings.

Nothing. In the starlight, it was hard to see.

Then a horse whinnied in the stables, and there was an explosion that blew windows at the near end of the stable out. Flames shot upward behind the broken glass. Then the night filled with the sounds of panic-stricken horses.

For a moment Jordan couldn't move. The horses. Brutus and Lucifer were in there. Cash had covered half the distance to the stables before she unfroze and tore after him. By the time she reached him, he had both palms pressed against the stable door. "It's hot. Stand back."

Once she had, he pulled the doors open, jumping back himself. Smoke and heat billowed out. Greedy flames began to lick their way up the frame as hooves crashed against stall doors. She recalled that Brutus was at this end, her father's horse at the other.

"I'll get Brutus," she said.

"No. Wait here. I can get them both."

The horses were shrieking now, and the flames had made their way to the top of the door frame. "There isn't time. I can handle Brutus."

"You'll have to take him out the far door. You'll never get him back through these flames."

"Go. We're wasting time."

He disappeared into the dark smoke that filled the building.

Jordan held her breath and kept her eyes straight ahead as she followed Cash. Out of the corner of her eye, she noted that the fire had taken hold in the stall to her left. Heat blasted at her as flames shot upward. When she had to take a breath, smoke stung her lungs. Just a few steps more. Brutus was in the next stall to her right.

"Brutus." She pitched her voice above the noise of the fire. "Brutus."

His only reply was to rear and shriek with fear.

Behind her, she could hear the fire growing, spreading, and a fit of coughing nearly overtook her. Wood splintered in the door of the stall. She felt her own panic; icy fingers of it clamped on her stomach like a vise. Ignoring it, she forced her mind to go cool. She had to act fast if she was going to save the horse.

Grabbing a blanket off a hook on the wall, she called Brutus's name again, then opened the door. He rushed past her, then reared in pure terror at the sight of the flames that now framed the doorway.

The second his hooves came down, she threw the blanket over his head and grabbed his halter rope. Screaming, he reared again. But the blanket stayed in place. When his hooves clattered to the floor a second time, she placed a hand on his neck and began to talk to him. A quick glance over her shoulder told her that the smoke had thickened. If she tried to lead him out the far end, the smoke could kill them before the fire could. Her best bet was to take Brutus out the way she'd come in.

She didn't let herself think about it anymore. Going on instinct, she moved her hand to where the tether rope circled his neck and half vaulted, half muscled her way onto Brutus's back. He reared again, but she held on. Then, holding tight to the rope and the ends of the blanket, she dug her heels into his flanks and sent up a prayer of thanks when he leaped forward.

For an instant, she knew what hell was like. The heat was intense, and fire reached out greedily on either side of them. Then they were out. Blanket and all, Brutus lunged forward. For the next few moments, she concentrated her attention on calming him. He ran blindly all the way to the ranch house before she was able to get him under control.

Still talking, she got the blanket off him and slid to the ground. Then she glanced back at the stables. The doorway she and Brutus had raced through was an inferno. Flames danced along the roof now, and an icy fear clawed through her. Had Cash gotten Lucifer out? Where were they?

CROUCHED LOW, Cash raced down the length of the stable. The fire wasn't as bad at this end, but the smoke surounded him. It had his eyes burning and his throat stinging. But he was very much aware that the fire behind him had started to roar.

Jordan.

Fear clawed at his gut, freezing him in his tracks. But when he turned, all he could see was an impenetrable wall of blackness. How was she going to get through that? A fit of coughing overtook him. Then the sound of a stall door splintering and Lucifer's frightened shrieking had him whirling and running toward the sound. He'd get the horse out first, then circle around the barn to help Jordan. There would be time. There had to be time.

He ran to the stable doors first and opened them. Smoke whooshed past him and the straw in the stall to his right burst into bright flames.

Behind him he heard Lucifer's hooves crash against his

stall door again. Cash reached him just as he lunged free. Eyes watering, he grabbed for the tether rope, then held tight as the panic-stricken horse reared and reared. Cash pointed the horse in the direction of the open door and slapped his flank.

Lucifer raced forward, and Cash tore after him. He had to get to Jordan, make sure that she was out. He'd cleared the stable door and had just reached the corner of the building when the blow struck him from behind. He saw stars before the ground came up to meet him.

PUSHING DOWN her fear, Jordan kept her eyes on the far side of the stables as she tied Brutus's tether rope to the railing on the front porch of the ranch. The moment she'd secured it, a familiar voice said, "Hello, Jordan."

She whirled so fast that Brutus whinnied and pulled at the tether. Raising a hand automatically to soothe the horse, she stared at her uncle Carleton. He was standing in the doorway to the ranch house, and he had a gun pointed at her.

14

"UNCLE CARLETON, what are you doing here?" Jordan asked.

"Technically, I'm in Phoenix attending a conference for investment bankers. Several people attended the talk I gave this afternoon. Others will vouch for the fact that I ate dinner with them. But actually I'm here because of Dorothy."

"I don't understand." Behind her the fire was roaring now, but she couldn't seem to take her eyes off the gun in her uncle's hand.

"When your mother became a problem for Dorothy, she took care of it on her own. She didn't even consult *me.*"

"You didn't know she killed Eva?"

"Heavens, no. Neither she nor Adam confided in me. We're not a particularly close family, and running Ware Bank takes all my time."

Her uncle's casual, careless tone had her blood chilling even further.

"However, Dorothy has inspired me to follow her example in this instance."

"You're the one who was working with Daniel Pearson. He was representing you?"

"No. He was representing Rainbow Limited, a charitable foundation that I established some time ago in Dorothy's name. I took care to make sure that he never dealt with me directly. They'll never trace him to me. Now, with the situation Dorothy is in, they'll probably be satisfied that she was pulling Pearson's strings. That part has worked out quite well."

"Why would Dorothy or you want the ranch?"

"For the turquoise mine, of course. It's worth a fortune. I learned about it years ago. Your mother let it slip once. Then she swore me to secrecy. Of course, I was already keeping a much bigger secret for her."

Jordan studied him. "You knew about Maddie all along. Did she tell you?"

"No." His voice took on an edge as he walked across the porch. Jordan had to keep herself from stepping back.

"I made it my business to find out exactly what my sister was doing when she deserted her duty to Ware Bank and ran away from home to pursue her frivolous dream. Keeping Maddie a secret gave me some real leverage over Eva for the first time. As long as I didn't say anything, Eva agreed to let me vote her stock at Ware Bank, make decisions on my own and live in Ware House. And that was only what was due me."

The edge in his voice had become angrier. Jordan had never seen her uncle express any kind of a heated emotion before.

"My father *should* have left the bank and the house to me." He gestured to his chest. "I was the oldest son. I was the one who shouldered the responsibility of running the bank. Eva ran away from all her rights to either of them when she went off to Santa Fe to study her *art*. Then when she returned, my father welcomed her like the prodigal son."

"But if you got everything you wanted by keeping my mother's secret, why do you need the turquoise mine?"

"Because Ware Bank is in trouble. Just temporary. A few unlucky calls on my part. All I need is a quick influx of cash to turn things around. I'd forgotten about the mine until Eva mentioned that Michael Farrell died. As I said, we weren't close but she seemed to need to tell someone, and I was the only option—fortunately for me. But Pearson was taking too long even after I offered a percentage of the future profits from the mine."

"So you hired someone to shoot at Maddie?"

"And to get rid of you."

His tone had calmed now and was almost sounding reasonable. It sent a new wave of chills through her.

"It all came to me while Fitzwalter was reading that will. Eva will never know how completely she solved all my problems. All I had to do was get rid of both of you, and the ranch would come to me as next of kin. Plus, I would have the added money that would come from the sale of Eva Ware Designs. My sister couldn't have played more completely into my hands."

"You won't be able to kill Maddie now. You'll be the prime suspect."

"Perhaps. But I would do anything to save Ware Bank. It's my duty, my responsibility. Eva would understand what I'm doing. She felt the same way about Eva Ware Designs."

Jordan doubted that her mother would have killed to preserve her life's work. But in an odd way, she thought her mother might understand her brother's absolute tunnel vision when it came to the family bank. Perhaps Mike Farrell would have understood it, too. Not the methods, but the intent.

Secrets. She'd thought before how good the Wares were at keeping them. Carleton, Dorothy and Adam had all been very good at hiding their true colors.

At least her parents, Mike and Eva, for all their faults, had never tried to hide what they were.

"Now, if you'll just come up and join me on the porch."

Brutus whinnied again and pulled at his tether. An answering whinny had Jordan turning to see Lucifer racing across the field beyond the stables.

Alone. There was no sign of Cash. Once more fear chilled her veins.

"If you're hoping that cowboy neighbor of Maddie's will rescue you, forget it. If he hasn't already, he'll die in the fire. One of my men will take care of that."

Jordan's heart nearly stopped. No, she wasn't going to let herself think about Cash right now. He could handle himself, and D.C. had only been minutes behind them in his car. He'd be here soon. Both men were smart and resourceful. So was she. And her job right now was to keep her uncle talking.

"Your men?"

"I brought two of them just to make sure. As you may have noticed, one of them is very skilled at setting fires. The other one is a pilot who flew us in on a small private plane. We'll be back in Phoenix in time for me to host a private party later tonight. Come now, Jordan. I don't like to be kept waiting."

Jordan stood her ground. "How did you know about Maddie's neighbor?"

"Pearson did manage to leave a rather detailed message about the guy sticking to you like glue, so we needed a distraction. And when he told me about another offer on the ranch, I knew I had to act fast. Now, it's really time for you to join me up here on the porch. I'm just going to knock you out until one of my men comes to take you to the barn. You and your neighbor are going to die tragically in the fire."

"No."

Carleton frowned at her. "Do as you're told, Jordan. Or I'll have to shoot you."

"You can't shoot me. I've met Detective Alvarez. He's a smart man and a friend of my *cowboy neighbor.* If I have a bullet in me, he'll know I didn't die accidentally. He'll track you down."

"If you don't come up here and join me, I'll shoot the horse."

Checkmate, Jordan thought. She stepped away from Brutus and began to walk toward her uncle. Once Brutus was safe, she was going to get that gun away from him.

THE PAIN in Cash's head was fierce. He welcomed it because as long as it was there, he was conscious. And his head wasn't the only pain he was experiencing. Someone had hold of his feet and was dragging him along the ground. Pebbles and stones bit into his back. He opened his eyes, blinked back tears and saw the blurred edge of the stable door, then the dark outline of the figure pulling him through it.

He closed his eyes and drew in a breath. His one advantage was that the air at ground level held more oxygen than the air at his opponent's level. Beyond his eyelids, he could see the brightness of the flames that had caught hold in the stall near the doorway. They weren't very far into the stables when the man dragging him began coughing and dropped his feet. Drawing back his foot, Cash gave him one hard clip to the kneecap.

The man fell like a tree, and Cash summoned all his strength, all his focus, to roll on top of him. Trying not to breathe, he grabbed the man's hair and smashed his face hard into the concrete floor of the stable. Once, then a second time. Afterwards, he rolled off and tried to stand. The flames were closer now, the smoke thicker. A fit of coughing overtook him.

"Need some help?"

Still crouching, Cash found the strength to swing a hand.

The man jumped back. "It's me. D.C. If you clip me in my good knee, neither one of us will get out of here."

"D.C.?"

"Yeah. If you can make it out on your own, I'll drag this guy."

They were both coughing as they staggered out of the stables. Once clear, D.C. dropped the body he'd been dragging next to another one.

"You've been…busy," Cash said.

"I knew the minute I saw the fire that something was up. So I ditched my car and climbed a few fences. Took your guy's pal out with my cane." D.C. retrieved it from the ground. "Are there any more?"

"Don't know. Have to help…Jordan. Left her…other end of the…stable."

"I saw her make it out on one of the horses."

Cash's relief was so intense his knees nearly buckled. "Got to…get to her."

Cash forced himself to take calm, even breaths. He wasn't going to be any good to anyone if he keeled over.

Together, they made their way along the stable wall. Cash spotted her first. She was standing near the front steps of the ranch house. The stars were bright enough that he saw the other figure, too—holding a gun.

His heart sank. There was absolutely no cover between the ranch house and the stables. If he and D.C. rushed the guy, he could easily shoot Jordan, then take them out like ducks in a shooting gallery.

"She's got his attention," D.C. said. "My brother claims she has a good head on her shoulders."

"She does." Remembering that helped Cash keep panic at bay. Brutus was tethered to the porch railing, and Jordan was standing close to him, her hand resting on his neck. They weren't close enough to hear what anyone was saying.

"How's your head?" D.C. asked.

"Fine. How's your leg?"

"Probably better than your head. If the man with the gun looks this way, we're right in his line of vision. So I figure our best bet is to angle our way to the bunkhouse. Then I'll circle around the far side of the ranch house and you take the shorter route to this side."

Cash pictured it in his mind. The trickiest part would be getting to the bunkhouse. But it was their best option. "And when we get to the house? He's got a gun. We don't."

D.C. shot him a grin. "I'll create a diversion and you take out the guy with the gun before he shoots me."

"How come you get the fun part?"

"See you in a few minutes." D.C. took off. Even with the limp, he was halfway to the bunkhouse before Cash started after him. He had to push the image of Jordan standing there facing a gun out of his mind. Instead, he concentrated on keeping his jog steady and his breathing even. Emotions would only slow him down. There'd be plenty of time for feeling later.

Once they were all safe.

By the time he reached the bunkhouse, D.C. had already started making his way to the far side of the ranch house.

Cash allowed himself the luxury of leaning against the wall for a moment. His mind cleared, and he didn't feel quite so breathless.

Still, he kept his jog slow. He couldn't risk another fit of coughing. When he reached his destination, he flattened his back against the wall and risked a quick look around the corner. Jordan had stepped away from Brutus and was talking calmly to a tall, distinguished gentleman in a business suit. Admiration mixed with fear as he watched her. There wasn't anything in her tone or demeanor to indicate that she was staring down the barrel of the gun.

Nor that the man holding it wasn't nearly as calm as she was.

Cash gauged his distance to the gunman. He'd need at least three, maybe four seconds to reach him. He prayed that D.C.'s diversion would last that long.

JORDAN STOPPED when she reached the foot of the porch steps. Out of the corner of her eye, she'd seen Cash look around the corner of the house.

He was safe. Relief mixed with fear because he was going to try to rush Uncle Carleton. She knew it. And heaven knew where the two men her uncle had hired were.

"One of my men should be here any minute."

He barely got the sentence out before there was a loud splintering sound and a section of the stable roof caved in.

"Bunglers." Carleton spit out the word in another sudden flash of fury. "I'm surrounded by idiots. They should have come to get you by now. You've got to be in that barn. Your death has to look like an accident." He descended a step. "I'm going to have to take care of this myself."

She had to calm him down. She wasn't sure the Uncle Carleton she'd always known was capable of using a gun. She was pretty sure the man pointing the gun at her right now was.

"Wait." Jordan raised a hand. "You haven't killed anyone yet, Uncle Carleton. Daniel Pearson acted on his own when he tried to kill Pete Blackthorn. Dorothy acted on her own to kill my mother. You could still walk away from all of this."

Okay, so he had hired professionals to do his killing for him. She wouldn't mention that.

"You don't understand," he said.

Jordan bit back a sigh of relief that the fury had faded a bit from his voice.

"I have to save Ware Bank. It was left in my care."

"I understand that. And Maddie and I can help with that. I can't believe my mother would have wanted the bank to fail."

"Your mother." He spat the words out. "She wouldn't have cared a fig if Ware Bank failed. And she wouldn't have lifted a finger to save it."

Jordan realized too late that she'd taken the wrong tack. She'd made him angry again.

"Enough. I'm through waiting. We're going to do this my way." He lunged down the steps toward her.

Even as she jumped back, Cash and D.C. raced around the corners of the house.

They both shouted something, and Carleton whirled in Cash's direction. He fired wildly once before Brutus neighed loudly and reared. It was the horse's descending hooves that knocked Carleton Ware to the ground.

Cash reached him first and kicked the gun away. Then Jordan rushed into his arms and held on tight.

"UNCLE CARLETON wanted to kill both of us." The shock and disbelief in Maddie's voice was a near perfect match to what Jordan was still feeling as she stood in the living room of the ranch with the phone pressed to her ear. The difference was that through the picture window, Jordan could see the spot where her uncle had stood on the porch the night before pointing the gun at her. She could also see the charred remains of the stables. And the lightning-fast images of Cash and D.C. rushing toward Carleton, of Brutus whinnying and rearing and knocking her uncle to the ground were still replaying themselves in her mind. If it hadn't been for Brutus, she might have lost Cash.

"But he didn't succeed." She turned and looked at Cash

and D.C., who were standing in the kitchen drinking coffee. They were safe. And so were Jase and Maddie now. The reality of that was slowly sinking in. Her uncle's injuries from his encounter with Brutus had been minor. He was refusing to talk, but Shay was confident that his accomplices would be more forthcoming.

Since it had been long after midnight by the time the detective had taken Carleton and his two henchmen into Santa Fe and Cash had arranged for Sweeney to transport the two horses to his ranch, she, Cash and D.C. had postponed calling New York with the latest news until morning. D.C. and Jase had spoken first. Then Cash had talked to Maddie. And now it was her turn to talk to her sister.

The sister she hadn't known existed until a week ago. Her knuckles white on the phone, Jordan shifted her gaze back to the window, to the land that stretched for miles until it gradually lifted into those hills, and something inside of her settled. A week ago, she hadn't known this place existed. She hadn't known Cash existed. So much had changed in her life so fast.

"He knew about us and the turquoise mine all these years," Maddie said. "And he never said a word."

"Keeping secrets seems to run in the Ware family," Jordan said.

"As far as secrets go," Maddie continued, "Mike Farrell was no slouch. Jase and I found a box in our mother's closet containing letters that he'd written to her over the years. She knew when I took my first step, when I cut my first tooth. He made sure she knew everything about me."

Jordan felt the rush of emotions, this time happy ones.

"And there was a letter to our father that she'd never mailed. It was dated just before he died. She wanted his permission to dissolve their bargain and bring us together.

Jase and I figure she found out that he'd passed, so she never mailed it. And she evidently couldn't find the courage to reunite us on her own. I'll bring everything once this twenty-one-day thing is over. And we'll search the ranch house. I'll bet our father has a box of photos stashed away somewhere, too."

When this twenty-one-day thing was over…

A little skip of fear moved up Jordan's spine. She glanced out to the kitchen again. Cash was standing, his hip against the counter, his long legs crossed at the ankles, his head tilted to one side as he listened intently to something D.C. was saying. Two days ago, she'd been so certain that when the three weeks were up, she'd be back in New York. So positive that her life, her responsibilities were there. Was she going to let herself be trapped by the same kind of tunnel vision and fear that her mother had?

Gripping the phone more tightly, she said, "I have news on this end, too. Pete Blackthorn knew about both of us all this time. He has a letter that our father addressed to both of us. He'll deliver it when you get here. And he told me why we were separated."

Jordan began to pace back and forth as she told her sister about the decision their parents had made all those years ago.

CASH WATCHED as Jordan paced, wishing he could do more to ease the burden of all she'd discovered in the past few days.

"She's a strong woman," D.C. said as he topped off Cash's mug and then refilled his own.

"So's Maddie," Cash said. "But they've got a lot on their plates. It's not only Eva Ware Designs and the ranch that they have to deal with. I'm betting they're going to have to take on Ware Bank's problems, too."

"Good thing they each have someone to lean on."

"Yes, they have each other."

"I was thinking of you and Jase."

Cash felt fear tighten in his belly. He'd nearly lost her twice yesterday. He didn't want to let himself think about the possibility that he might lose her again in eighteen days. "For now."

D.C. turned to him, studied him for a moment. "You don't impress me as a man who's slow off the mark."

"What?"

"Life's short. If I had a woman looking at me the way Jordan looks at you and I felt the same way, I wouldn't wait eighteen days to stake my claim. If you don't mind a bit of free advice, you could use the dude ranch thing as leverage—if you wanted to persuade her to stay here instead of returning to New York. She's really into it. I have half a mind to put her in touch with the real Greg Majors."

"Everything's happened so fast," Cash said.

"It's happened fast for Jase and Maddie, too. But I've seen the way my brother looks at her. And he's got that business background in common with Jordan. I'll bet he's already making plans—maybe to open a branch of his business out here in Santa Fe."

Cash looked back at Jordan. She was still talking to Maddie, and she'd paused in front of the window to look out at the land her father had sent her away from. He'd wanted to give her time, to give them both time, but she looked so right standing there.

Suddenly, all his nerves settled. They might come from different worlds, different backgrounds, but she was right for him, too. It was just that simple. Just that true. Now all he had to do was convince Jordan of that.

D.C. set his mug down on the counter. "Well, I think my work here is done. I'm going to pack up and get out of your hair. I'll stop on my way to the airport and get the latest update from your friend Alvarez."

Cash nodded absently, never once taking his gaze off of Jordan as D.C. left the room.

IT WAS LATE AFTERNOON when Jordan and Cash urged their horses up the last incline to the top of the bluff. Once D.C. had left, Cash had talked her into letting him complete that tour of the ranch he'd promised her—was it only two days ago? He'd driven her over to his place and had barely said a word. Then he'd given her a whirlwind tour of his home while Sweeney had saddled Brutus and Cash's horse, Mischief.

His housekeeper had packed them some food and they'd ridden off toward the canyon that joined the two ranches. The ride had been fast and hard, and it should have cleared her mind. But she'd felt wired from the moment that D.C. had driven off toward Santa Fe. It was as if a clock were ticking and time was slipping away from her.

At some point while talking to her sister, she'd come to a decision. Now all she had to do was share it with Cash. She'd made business presentations hundreds of times. She knew how to persuade people. So why was she ten times more nervous than she'd been representing Maddie's jewelry at that show yesterday?

When the horses reached a level piece of land, Cash turned Mischief around and Jordan followed suit.

"I brought you here because I wanted you to see this."

Jordan looked around and simply absorbed the view. The land fell away on either side of the hills, pristine and breathtaking in its beauty. In spite of the shimmering heat, she could make out the miniature buildings of the two ranches. With the exception of those structures, nothing marred the landscape.

"I see now why my father didn't want anyone to know about the turquoise mine. No matter how much money he could have made, it wouldn't have been worth it."

Cash smiled at her. At her count, it was the first one he'd given her all day, and something inside of her eased a bit.

"I'm sorry he didn't live to meet you."

Jordan felt her throat tighten. "Me, too. But you're showing me a lot about him. And I'll learn more." She shifted her gaze to the land again, knowing that it was an integral part of her father. "In the city, there aren't any places like this where I can get away and just breathe. Maddie told me that this place was special—that I would find something here."

And she had. She turned to Cash. It wasn't just the land. It was the man. They came from different worlds just as her parents had. Like her mother, she was a New Yorker. Like her father, he was a rancher who loved the wide-open spaces.

When he placed a hand over hers on the pommel of the saddle, she glanced down and saw the sharp contrast. His fingers were larger, his palm callused, and yet somehow they fit. She met his eyes. There were so many differences between them and yet she felt the pull—sure, steady and right. And she felt her heart drop just as fast and hard as if it had fallen off the ledge in front of them.

"I also brought you here for another reason, Jordan," Cash said.

"I figured. To seduce me." She tried a tentative smile, but he didn't return it.

"We'll get to that. But first I have something to say."

"Me, too." Ignoring the flutter of panic in her stomach, Jordan hurried on. "I was wrong."

For a moment his hand tightened on hers. "About what?"

"About us."

His eyes narrowed and the intensity of his gaze nearly had her throat drying up. She could do this. She had to do this. "I was wrong about the ground rules I set up at the very beginning of this…relationship. I thought I knew what I wanted—a mutually enjoyable time that we could both walk away from in twenty-one days. No harm, no foul. But I've changed my mind."

When he said nothing, she lifted her chin. "A woman has a right to do that."

"It depends. What have you changed it to?"

Without knowing exactly how, Jordan found her fingers had become linked with his. "I want more time."

"Why?" he asked again.

Panic fluttered again, but she shoved it down. "Because I need it. Because I think what we're discovering together deserves it. And I don't want to make the same mistake my mother did. I understand now that she walked away from my father and from Maddie because she was so focused on her goal of creating a successful jewelry empire that she couldn't see that she could have had that and more. When I thought that I had to go back to New York and make sure that her legacy lived on, I was being as blind as she was. I want more. I need more."

"Why?"

Jordan swallowed hard. "Because I really want to develop a business plan for the dude ranch, and I want to be here a lot of the time to run it. I can still oversee the business side of Eva Ware Designs. And I want to help Maddie, too. I don't want her to merely step into the job of head designer at Eva Ware Designs. She can do that if she wants, but she has her own reputation to build. I'm going to encourage her to do that. And then there's Ware Bank."

He gave her a brief nod. Whether it was approval or disapproval, she wasn't sure.

"There's no excuse for what my uncle did or tried to do, but I do understand his desire to keep a family business running. But I don't have to be in New York all the time to help out with that."

"You're nervous. You always talk a lot when you're nervous. So I don't think you've gotten yet to the real reason you want to change the ground rules. Give me the bottom line, Jordan. Why?"

She felt a sudden flare of anger and tamped down on it. Because he was right. And she was stalling. She studied him sitting there on his horse, and it wasn't some fantasy she saw. It was Cash Landry. And suddenly she knew.

Meeting his eyes steadily, she said, "I want to change the ground rules because I want more than twenty-one days with you. Because I love you."

He raised their joined hands to his lips in a gesture that had her heart tumbling again. "Same goes." He smiled that slow easy smile. "I know how much you like to map things out and see where you're headed. So how much more time are you thinking of?"

The mix of heat and amusement she saw in his eyes had her stomach settling. It reminded her of exactly what she'd seen that first morning she'd woken up in bed with him.

"I was thinking of a lifetime."

He pulled her close then, and when his mouth was only a breath away from hers, he murmured, "I hope you're open to negotiations. I brought you out here to convince you we'd need two lifetimes. Maybe more."

"Deal."

Then he kissed her.

Brutus whinnied, Mischief pawed the ground. But Jordan held on tight.

She'd come home.

Epilogue

Eighteen days later

THE SUN had begun its descent behind the mountains south-west of the ranch as Cash stirred the coals in the barbecue pit. They were just beginning to turn white at the edges.

"Let me know when you're ready for the steaks," Jase said.

Cash glanced over to the corral near the new stable. Maddie and Jordan sat together on the top rung of the fence watching Julius Caesar and Brutus take each other's measure. Jordan had arranged for Julius Caesar to be shipped across country, timing his arrival to coincide with Jase's and Maddie's yesterday.

The women's heads were close, and in the slanting sunlight they made a pretty picture. "I think the ladies will let us know when they're hungry."

Jase followed the direction of Cash's gaze, then reached into a cooler and pulled out two beers. "If we leave it entirely up to them, we won't be eating those steaks until breakfast."

Cash took a long swallow of the beer Jase handed him. "They stayed up all night talking. You'd think they'd run out of things to say."

Jase's brows arched upward. "I've never known Jordan to be at a loss for words. And the two of them have a life-time to catch up on."

"True." Cash smiled slowly. "With Jordan at the helm, they have another lifetime to plan."

Jase chuckled. "I see you're getting to know her. But I imagine Maddie will get her two cents' worth in. She went to bat for her cousin, Adam, and convinced Jordan that they shouldn't press charges for the robbery if Adam agreed to get help for his gambling problem. The D.A. was agreeable as long as Adam promised to testify against the loan shark he borrowed so much money from. I think Maddie felt sorry for him."

"And Jordan probably saw it as a good business decision because she believes him to be a talented designer. Without pressure from his mother, he might turn into an asset at Eva Ware Designs."

"They're going to make a good team." Jase turned to Cash. "By the way, I owe you one."

"What for?"

"Those karate moves you taught Maddie. One of them saved my life. Hers, too."

Cash smiled at him. "Then it was time well spent." He glanced at his coals. "Ten more minutes and we're going to have to round 'em up and bring 'em in. I'll open a bottle of chardonnay as bait and we'll take them a couple of glasses along with the letter Pete Blackthorn delivered while they were riding."

"Good plan."

"I've got another one. Tonight, I'm taking Jordan back to my place. That will give you and Maddie some privacy."

Jase studied Cash. "If you can pull that off, you're going to be my new best friend."

"Watch and learn. I know just what bait to use then, too. Making love in the back of my pickup is on our to-do list."

Jase raised his beer bottle in a toast. "I like your style."

"I'M STILL TRYING to get my mind around the other Wares," Maddie said. "I knew from the time I met them that there was something different about them."

"Different is way too mild a word. Carleton was absolutely nuts. I saw it in his eyes. I'm amazed he was able to hide it all these years."

Maddie shivered a little. "I saw it in Dorothy's eyes, too."

"At least Adam might be salvageable," Jordan mused. "I think you're right about him. He's a lot like our mother—focused on his career as a designer. I think she saw a lot of herself in him. That may be why she didn't want to prosecute him when she discovered he robbed the store. And the gambling may have been his way of acting out against his mother's constant derision and dissatisfaction."

"Our mother may have had some faults, but they were light years away from Dorothy Ware's." Maddie glanced at Jordan. "I have a question about Eva."

"Ask away."

"Are you angry with her for what she did? I mean, she didn't want either one of us, and then she was the one who insisted that we never know about each other."

Jordan shook her head. "I'm not angry at all. She may have been the cause of our separation, but in the end she brought us together." Jordan let her gaze sweep the landscape. "And in the end she opened up new worlds for me. Not just this place, but all the new business challenges I'm finding here."

"I feel the same way about New York and about working at Eva Ware Designs. I'm learning so much from helping Cho to finish her designs. I can't help but feel grateful to her."

Jordan glanced over her shoulder and saw the two men walking toward them. "If it hadn't been for the terms of our mother's will, I never would have found Cash."

"And I never would have found Jase. We owe her big-time."

"We come bearing gifts," Cash said as he reached them. Jase handed them each a glass of wine and Cash handed Jordan the letter. "Pete Blackthorn brought this while you were out riding."

Jordan looked down at the script—*Maddie and Jordan*—and she ran a finger over the writing.

"This is the letter you told me about," Maddie said. "Read it to us."

Jordan nodded as she broke the seal and held it so that Maddie could see.

Dear Maddie and Jordan,

If you're reading this, it means that you're together at last—something that I didn't live long enough to see. I'm also hoping it means that the gamble I took when I kept the daughter who even at six months loved to play with shiny stones and sent away the daughter who loved to ride with me on my horse has paid off and played some part in your finding one another.

Enjoy one another as I've enjoyed watching both of you grow up.

All my love,
Dad

Jordan reached for Maddie's hand and held on. "He mixed us up on purpose."

"Because he loved us and he hoped we'd be together one day."

"Hear! Hear!" Cash raised his glass in a toast. "To Mike Farrell."

"And to Eva Ware," Maddie said as she lifted her glass.

"To our parents," Jordan said.

And all four of them drank.

* * * * *

Celebrate 60 years of pure reading pleasure with Harlequin!

To commemorate the event, Harlequin Intrigue® is thrilled to invite you to the wedding of The Colby Agency's J. T. Baxley and his bride, Eve Mattson.

That is, of course, if J.T. can find the woman who left him at the altar. Considering he's a private investigator for one of the top agencies in the country—the best of the best—that shouldn't be a problem. The real setback is that his bride isn't who she appears to be…and her mysterious past has put them both in danger.

Enjoy an exclusive glimpse of Debra Webb's latest addition to
THE COLBY AGENCY: ELITE RECONNAISSANCE DIVISION

THE BRIDE'S SECRETS

Available August 2009 from Harlequin Intrigue®.

The dark figures on the dock were still firing. The bullets cutting through the surface of the water without the warning boom of shots told Eve they were using silencers.

That was to her benefit. Silencers decreased the accuracy of every shot and lessened the range.

She grabbed for the rocks. Scrambled through the darkness. Bumped her knee on a boulder. Cursed.

Burrowing into the waist-deep grass, she kept low and crawled forward. Faster. Pushed harder. Needed as much distance as possible.

Shots pinged on the rocks.

J.T. scrambled alongside her.

He was breathing hard.

They had to stay close to the ground until they reached the next row of warehouses. Even though she was relatively certain they were out of range at this point, she wasn't taking any risks. And she wasn't slowing down.

J.T. had to keep up.

The splat of a bullet hitting the ground next to Eve had her rolling left. Maybe they weren't completely out of range.

She bumped J.T. He grunted.

His injured arm. Dammit. She could apologize later.

Half a dozen more yards.

Almost in the clear.

As she reached the cover of the alley between the first two warehouses she tensed.

Silence.

No pings or splats.

She glanced back at the dock. Deserted.

Time to run.

Her car was parked another block down.

Pushing to her feet, she sprinted forward. The wet bag dragged at her shoulder. She ignored it.

By the time she reached the lot where her car was parked, she had dug the keys from her pocket and hit the fob. Six seconds later she was behind the wheel. She hit the ignition as J.T. collapsed into the passenger seat. Tires squealed as she spun out of the slot.

"What the hell did you do to me?"

From the corner of her eye she watched him shake his head in an attempt to clear it.

He would be pissed when she told him about the tran-quilizer.

She'd needed him cooperative until she formulated a plan. A drug-induced state of unconsciousness had been the fastest and most efficient method to ensure his continued solidarity.

"I can't really talk right now." Eve weaved into the right lane as the street widened to four lanes. What she needed was traffic. It was Saturday night—shouldn't be that difficult to find as soon as they were out of the old warehouse district.

A glance in the rearview mirror warned that their unwanted company had caught up.

Sensing her tension, J.T. turned to peer over his left shoulder.

"I hope you have a plan B."

She shot him a look. "There's always plan G." Then she pulled the Glock out of her waistband.

Cutting the steering wheel left, she slid between two vehicles. Another veer to the right and she'd put several cars between hers and the enemy.

She was betting they wouldn't pull out the firepower in the open like this, but a girl could never be too sure when it came to an unknown enemy.

Deep blending was the way to go.

Two traffic lights ahead the marquis of a movie theater provided exactly the opportunity she was looking for.

The digital numbers on the dash indicated it was just past midnight. Perfect timing. The late movie would be purging its audience into the crowd of teenagers who liked hanging out in the parking lot.

She took a hard right onto the property that sported a twelve-screen theater, numerous fast-food hot spots and a chain superstore. Speeding across the lot, she selected a lane of parking slots. Pulling in as close to the theater entrance as possible, she shut off the engine and reached for her door.

"Let's go."

Thankfully he didn't argue.

Rounding the hood of her car, she shoved the Glock into her bag, then wrapped her arm around J.T.'s and merged into the crowd.

With her free hand she finger-combed her long hair. It was soaked, as were her clothes. The kids she bumped into noticed, gave her death-ray glares.

They just didn't know.

As she and J.T. moved in closer to the building, she grabbed a baseball cap from an innocent bystander. The crowd made it easy. The kid who owned the cap had made it even easier by stuffing the cap bill-first into his waist-band at the small of his back.

Pushing through the loitering crowd, she made her way

to the side of the building next to the main entrance. She pushed J.T. against the wall and dropped her bag to the ground. Peeled off her tee and let it fall.

His gaze instantly zeroed in on her breasts, where the cami she wore had glued to her skin like an extra layer. A zing of desire shot through her veins.

Not the time.

With a flick of her wrist she twisted her hair up and clamped the cap atop the blonde mass.

"They're coming," J.T. muttered as he gazed at some point beyond her.

"Yeah, I know." She planted her palms against the wall on either side of him and leaned in. "Keep your eyes open. Let me know when they're inside."

Then she planted her lips on his.

* * * * *

Will J.T. and Eve be caught in the moment?
Or will Eve get the chance to reveal all of her secrets?
Find out in
THE BRIDE'S SECRETS
by Debra Webb
Available August 2009 from Harlequin Intrigue®

HARLEQUIN
60 YEARS
of pure reading pleasure

We'll be spotlighting a different series every month
throughout 2009 to celebrate our 60th anniversary.

LOOK FOR
HARLEQUIN INTRIGUE®
IN AUGUST!

COLBY AGENCY
ELITE RECONNAISSANCE DIVISION

To commemorate the event, Harlequin Intrigue® is thrilled
to invite you to the wedding of the Colby Agency's
J.T. Baxley and his bride, Eve Mattson.

Look for *Colby Agency: Elite Reconnaissance*

THE BRIDE'S SECRETS
BY DEBRA WEBB

Available August 2009

www.eHarlequin.com

HIBPA09

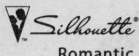

You're invited to join our Tell Harlequin Reader Panel!

By joining our new reader panel you will:

- Receive Harlequin® books—they are FREE and yours to keep with no obligation to purchase anything!
- Participate in fun online surveys
- Exchange opinions and ideas with women just like you
- Have a say in our new book ideas and help us publish the best in women's fiction

In addition, you will have a chance to win great prizes and receive special gifts! See Web site for details. Some conditions apply. Space is limited.

To join, visit us at

www.TellHarlequin.com.

THBPA0108

REQUEST YOUR FREE BOOKS!

2 FREE NOVELS
PLUS 2
FREE GIFTS!

HARLEQUIN®

Blaze™

Red-hot reads!

YES! Please send me 2 FREE Harlequin® Blaze™ novels and my 2 FREE gifts (gifts are worth about $10). After receiving them, if I don't wish to receive any more books, I can return the shipping statement marked "cancel". If I don't cancel, I will receive 6 brand-new novels every month and be billed just $4.24 per book in the U.S. or $4.71 per book in Canada. That's a savings of 15% off the cover price. It's quite a bargain. Shipping and handling is just 50¢ per book.* I understand that accepting the 2 free books and gifts places me under no obligation to buy anything. I can always return a shipment and cancel at any time. Even if I never buy another book, the two free books and gifts are mine to keep forever.

151 HDN EYS2   351 HDN EYTE

Name	(PLEASE PRINT)
Address	Apt. #
City State/Prov.	Zip/Postal Code

Signature (if under 18, a parent or guardian must sign)

Mail to the **Harlequin Reader Service:**
IN U.S.A.: P.O. Box 1867, Buffalo, NY 14240-1867
IN CANADA: P.O. Box 609, Fort Erie, Ontario L2A 5X3

Not valid to current subscribers of Harlequin Blaze books.

Want to try two free books from another line?
Call 1-800-873-8635 or visit www.morefreebooks.com.

* Terms and prices subject to change without notice. Prices do not include applicable taxes. N.Y. residents add applicable sales tax. Canadian residents will be charged applicable provincial taxes and GST. Offer not valid in Quebec. This offer is limited to one order per household. All orders subject to approval. Credit or debit balances in a customer's account(s) may be offset by any other outstanding balance owed by or to the customer. Please allow 4 to 6 weeks for delivery. Offer available while quantities last.

Your Privacy: Harlequin Books is committed to protecting your privacy. Our Privacy Policy is available online at www.eHarlequin.com or upon request from the Reader Service. From time to time we make our lists of customers available to reputable third parties who may have a product or service of interest to you. If you would .prefer we not share your name and address, please check here. ☐

HB09R3

COMING NEXT MONTH

Available July 28, 2009

#483 UNBRIDLED Tori Carrington
After being arrested for a crime he didn't commit, former Marine Carter Southard is staying far away from the one thing that's always gotten him into trouble—women! Unfortunately, his sexy new attorney, Laney Cartwright, is making that very difficult....

#484 THE PERSONAL TOUCH Lori Borrill
Professional matchmaker Margot Roth needs to give her latest client the personal touch—property mogul Clint Hilton is a playboy extraordinaire and is looking for a date...for his mother. But while Margot's setting up mom, Clint decides Margot's for him. Let the seduction begin!

#485 HOT UNDER PRESSURE Kathleen O'Reilly
Where You Least Expect It
Ashley Larsen and David McLean are hot for each other. Who knew the airport would be the perfect place to find the perfect sexual partner? But can the lust last when it's a transcontinental journey every time these two want to hook up?

#486 SLIDING INTO HOME Joanne Rock
Encounters
Take me out to the ball game... Four sexy major leaguers are duking it out for the ultimate prize—the Golden Glove award. Little do they guess that the women fate puts in their path will offer them even more of a challenge...and a much more satisfying reward!

#487 STORM WATCH Jill Shalvis
Uniformly Hot!
During his stint in the National Guard, Jason Mauer had seen his share of natural disasters. But when he finds himself in a flash flood with an old crush—sexy Lizzy Mann—the waves of desire turn out to be too much....

#488 THE MIGHTY QUINNS: CALLUM Kate Hoffmann
Quinns Down Under
Gemma Moynihan's sexy Irish eyes are smiling on Callum Quinn! Charming the ladies has never been quiet Cal's style. But he plans to charm the pants off luscious Gemma—until he finds out she's keeping a dangerous secret...

www.eHarlequin.com

HBCNMBPA0709